For Tom, the best brother I could have asked for.

And for my grandparents, always supporting that crazy kid.

Acknowledgments

Too many people are needed to be thanked for any book. Especially a first. First off to my editor and greatest person ever, Sherrie Hall. Could not get through any day without you. Russell Nohelty, guiding the entirety of Arcane Inkdustries through its first year, and always available for comment and critique both as an artist and businessman.

To the artists, Phoebe, Saint, James, Cari, Ed, Carlos. You each contributed just as much as I did. The indie community online always deserves the respect it gets, and a lot more it doesn't. Special regards to Bob Salley, Kelly Bender, Alex Maday Kevin Parent, for their support and words of encouragement.

To Gregory Maguire, a man amongst writers who listened to one kid in church ask him too many questions over too many years.

To my family, both extremely supportive and always a soft reminder that writing comes after dishes.

And last, of course, to you, dear reader. I hope you enjoy this work as much as I did in the creation. Just holding it in your hands is the greatest compliment you could ever give me.

— *Jack Holder*

THIS BOOK BELONGS TO

Kailyn Martorilli

Table of Contents

Acknowledgments v

Introduction viii

The First Generation

Promethean Sparks 1

Cheating Spells 16

Mars: Year 1 18

Post-Apocalyptic Flooding 31

Adapted Armaments, The Last Bullet 45

Poetry

Magical Poetry 56

3 Spells gone Awry 56

A New Path 58

Spell Song 58

Lich's Lament 59

Sonnets 60

Running through Time

Lost Heroines 61

Lost Heroines, Namesake 76

Proper War
(or How Blood Feuds should never interrupt Dinner Plans) 91

A Family Far Beneath the Stars 109

The Ax Rises 122

A Girl and her Goddess 133

The Mad Fiddler 142

A Prayer for the Thirteen 151

The Artists

Thank You to our Generous Backers

Mike Burke	Tom Holder
Katharine Clarke	Jami Ann Kravec
Tina Clarke	Bart Kuiper
Marcus Currie	Mary Jane Lloyd
Lynn Hall	Alex Maday
Mark Hall	Doug MacLellan
Sherrie Hall	Scearly

Introduction

When I think of Jack, I can't help but thinking about Facebook.

Jack and I met because of a Kickstarter campaign. I gave him some advice about how to add momentum to a stalled campaign. I like to believe it's what got his campaign funded in the end, but that might be my oversized ego. Since then, I would randomly get these little Facebook messages every week or so saying things like "Hope you are having a great day!", "Congrats on doing a thing!", and the like.

I'll be honest, they were annoying at first, mostly because I knew in my bones he was prepping me for some huge favor. People are always prepping me for some huge favor.

I waited and waited, but the favor never came.

Jack just really wanted to know what was going on in my life. He was kind, polite, funny, and insightful. He still is to this day. I mean, unless Bizarro Jack from an alternate dimension took his place. If you meet Jack and he's not polite and courteous, be wary. It's probably an imposter.

Despite myself, I grew to really like Jack as a person. I knew he was a writer, but he never talked about it much. He toiled in the background, cranking out things but mostly we just chatted. He never asked me to read his work, or review it, or help him in any way. Well, until he asked me to write this introduction. Touché, Jack. Touché. I supposed you were prepping me for that huge favor all along.

When he started posting this short story collection online, I cringed. It's not because I thought he was a bad writer. It's because almost nobody is a good writer. I don't mean a competent writer. Tons of people are competent writers. I mean a really good, engaging writer. Even fewer elevate themselves into the realm of storyteller, and with fantasy stories you must be able to spin a good yarn.

I liked Jack. You can tell I really like Jack because I'm writing this introduction for him. I didn't want to hate his work. That would quickly sour our relationship. Nobody likes to be told they suck at the thing they love, and I hate lying to people.

I waited with bated breath when he posted that first story. I didn't want to read it. If I never read it, I wouldn't have to destroy the nice, cozy friendship bubble we created. I liked my illusion, but friendship is about reality. I had to read it.

So I clenched my body tight, prepared for torture, and dug in...but the torture never came. His stories were good, like really good. Not just good for a friend, but good for any writer. They aren't just technically good either, they are enjoyable, fresh, and innovative. They are filled with pathos, and humor, and drama, and intrigue. They are just great stories.

I kept reading and reading, thinking I would find a bad one in the batch, but I didn't. I should thank Jack for restoring a little bit of my faith in writers. I should definitely thank him for restoring some of my faith in humanity.

If you picked up this book because you love Jack, you are in for a treat because it's a really, really good book. If you are clenching your teeth because you don't want to pop your own bubble, you can relax.

If you are standing in a book store, or his convention table, or with your Kindle trying to decide whether to pluck down a few shekels on this book, just know that I wouldn't be writing these words unless the book was awesome.

Seriously, when Jack asked me to write this introduction my first instinct was "Christ. I don't wanna do that." But when I read the proof copy, I grew to love them again. I remembered my own story of Jack and I wanted to commemorate it forever.

I suppose what I'm trying to say is buy the book already. You'll find something inside its pages to love. If you don't, at least you helped one of the last decent human beings in the world level up.

Now enough about me. Let's get on with the book already.

- Russell Nohelty
Writer, publisher, fan

Russell Nohelty is the creator and owner of Wannabe Press. His works include "Spaceship Broken, Needs Repairs," "Ichabod Jones: Monster Hunter," and "My Father Didn't Kill Himself." You can find his work at www.wannabepress.com

Promethean Sparks

"Spells. Sparks. That's how the story starts."

Professor Metteus ended his class every day with the exact same words. They didn't seem to be a quotation, or even have some deep meaning. Certainly the man never explained the words or why he said them every day. Every day, just like this one, he would lean against the front of the desk, stare ahead into the class, and wait. He would almost expect an answer to a question that he never said.

Why he expected an answer was beyond the knowledge of the class. Professor Metteus was one of the teachers you certainly listened to, but actually talking never really seemed to be an option. He wasn't loud, boisterous, he truly wasn't anything.

Except spindly. He had to hobble about on a cane, and his hands most often shook whenever handing back a paper or test. A stick figure would have more definition than Professor Metteus.

After a few moments of silence, Professor Metteus bowed his head, and returned to his seat. He settled into the armchair, picked up a pen, and stared at the wooden furniture.

"Maybe next time," He whispered under his breath.

"Have a wonderful day," He said to the class as they filed out. The professor closed his eyes, and turned off the world for a moment.

One student remained in his seat, and pondered his choices. Brian wanted to answer the question. Truly. If nothing else, it seemed important. Not just to Metteus, but to him. He wanted to know what kind of story needed a spark. Or maybe if it was the one he was looking for.

"Professor Metteus?"

The professor looked up.

"Brian? Yes?"

Brian scuffed the floor with his shoes. Come on, he whispered o himself. This isn't high school, this is college, dammit.

"The stories that you have us reading."

"What about them?"

"Aren't they, you know..." Brian winced. "Dark?"

Professor Metteus grabbed his cane, and lifted himself up. "Dark?"

"Well, we've read all these classics, and they never seem to have a happy ending." Brian started to count them off. "Everyone dies in Hamlet and MacBeth, Frankenstein creates a monster, To

Kill a Mockingbird ends with innocence dying so racists can be content..."

"Yes."

Brian waited for a moment. "Well?"

"Well what?"

"Well that isn't right!"

Professor Metteus shrugs. "We discussed this in the beginning of class, Brian. Literature is not just a set of stories, but an early cinematic experience that served as explanations for morality and the human experience and you have already tuned me out, haven't you?"

He didn't mean to, but Brian couldn't think straight. This wasn't what he was studying classics for. The boy in him remembered good tales, grew up with them.

Professor Metteus shook his head, and clenched his eyes shut.

"What do you want, son?"

"I want the boy's adventures to come back!" Brian shouted.

They stared at each other.

"What?"

"These story, things," Brian shook around the room. "It's always happening. Everything is about the apocalypse, or zombies, or Ragnarok and the end of days. Since the beginning of time we have only been concerned with the ending, except for a boy's adventure."

The corner of Metteus' mouth twitched. If it was a smile, he didn't allow it to grow any further.

"Telling stories is something of a specialty of mine," The professor said. "There are stories with happy endings."

"They aren't any good." Any good, Brian was sounding like a kid. And why not? The world treated students as such, and they thought of themselves that way. To be honest, this student thought of himself as a child. And children do not respect the social niceties, so onward and forward!

"Then do better," Professor Metteus sat in one of the desks, and looked at Brian. "Tell me what a good boy's story needs."

"Adventure!" Brian said. "Dashing over forest and mountain stream, up the crags and down the waterfalls. Fighting goblins,"

"Goblins?" Metteus' eyebrows rose. "I thought this was a Greek myth."

"Who said it was a Greek myth?" Brian was working himself up in this, and wasn't going to let anything like logic disrupt his thought process. "This has goblins and giants, kings and dragons."

"Let's not involve the dragons yet." Professor Metteus stood up. "And I'm assuming the good guy will win in the end?"

"Of course," Brian said. "But it can't be certain."

Metteus frowned. "How can a certain ending not be certain?"

"Because a certain ending is for matters of science and the classroom." Brian could almost see his thought running out of his head. In the classroom, X=X, 2+2=4, etc. There was a logical conclusion given a set of facts and situations, which could be easily predicted.

Not so with a story. Even if 4 is the logical conclusion, it would never be something so simple as two and two put together. Because two and two would be twenty-two, divided by fire and squared by the root of all evil. That is how a story finds its way to and fro, or to two and four.

"You're rambling."

Had Brian said that aloud? He couldn't remember. Did it matter? Where was he?

"Focus. So we have a giant to fight, and goblins and all manners of darkness." Metteus looked out into the encroaching black. It spilled out of the blackboard, tendrils almost reaching out of the green in hunger. It reached towards the two of them. "I hope you realize that even when the outcome seems certain, even a child risks his life when he goes on an adventure."

Brian could only nod. He must be dreaming.

"We have the beginnings of a good story, with a good ending," Metteus yelled. The darkness was joined by a howling wind that tore into their clothes. Metteus' jacket whipped open, revealing a blood-red shirt underneath. Brian huddled within himself and tried to consider what was happening.

"Once upon a time," Metteus muttered. "A time that was now, and will be again. We may not know how, but we will be then." He was so stunned that he must be speaking in simple rhymes.

"What is this story about?"

Brian looked around himself. Professor Metteus was gone. There was nothing, only black. Wind howled out of nowhere.

"The page is blank, storyteller. Give it some life. Give it a soul. Who is the hero?"

"A, a young boy, about twelve years old..."

"Don't just start there," Metteus warned. "If this is a real tale, describe him."

Describe him? Well, he has a young face. *Stop saying young.* A voice echoed through the black. *Young is nothing more than an age of foolishness.*

No, the boy has a youthful face. Look there, as he glances from one spot to a next. He takes everything in. The smallest smile is on his face, almost wanting permission to grow. A mess of hair, the color of sand on straw, is plastered on his head. Sweat-soaked and panting from running to his favorite spot. Peeking out of the hair are freckles, stretching from cheek to cheek across a rounded nose. Strange, Brian always had freckles as a kid.

He jumps onto a rock. Short, thin. That boy could probably have a better time scrambling up the rock if he dropped that stick of his. But it is his favorite, just the right heft and length. Two-thirds the length of his arm, and as wide around as a baseball bat, he could tell all sorts of stories about that stick. And get in trouble with no end of people.

That is a young boy. *Is it good?* No, because good is not a concept yet. Good is done, because what else is there? He jokes, I run through the woods.

What are you wearing? I'm wearing my favorite blue shirt. *Blue? Not red?* Red is okay, and has its place. But blue is for boys. Blue shirt, ragged at the elbows, and brown pants that are green at the knees.

What is your name?

"My name is Bree," The boy whispered.

He looked around, and light started to poke out of the black. He frowned, and scratched that sandy straw hair out of his eyes. He was confused. Was he Brian, or Bree? After a moment, he probably thought he was both, though it was Bree's turn to play.

Professor Metteus' body was gone. He didn't seem to be, Bree could almost feel him pressing on the background. The professor lay just behind the scenes, waiting to be recognized.

Where are you?

Where was Bree? He was in the forest of Anworth, of course! This was his second home. Look to the east, and the sun is rising up over the mountain valley on the trees. The firs mixed with the oaks and maples. If he turned just so, Bree could feel the air. Ah, that smell. The firs mixed in with brine from the sea, swirling through the mountain valley. Bree could stay here forever.

Any people? Of course there were people. Go over the northern mountain, and you would come to the village of Greenshere. The most peaceful den of villains to be found in all the lands. Proper villains, that only attacked either during daytime, or right after dinner so as to not ruin a meal. Any other time and they were more than willing to give directions to their favorite fishing spots or a fruit tree that just recently ripened.

Bree could hear a laughter crackle next to him. *It seems a perfect danger.* It was. Everything a boy could ask for. Bandits, cutthroats, even pirates. Though the goblins were a trouble.

Did Bree think goblins? Where did the goblins come from? There they were, peeking out from behind that fallen oak tree. Bree counted five as they emerged. They were a mottled green, with squat heads on spindled bodies. They held onto their daggers for dear life, almost thrust out ahead of them in surrender.

As they recognized that this was a boy, the goblins stopped. They smiled, and relaxed. Perhaps an adventurer was too much for them, but a boy might be a different matter.

Bree held his stick forward, and glared straight ahead. He was the hero, he's got this. He's also apparently twelve and couldn't remember anything about combat other than running and hiding.

You should probably do that. That sounded like a wonderful idea. Bree turned and ran towards the mountains.

The boy could hear the goblins behind him. Keep running, just keep running. Bree fell into the boy's memories. His footsteps became more familiar, more practiced. He had run over these woods every day of his life. Every night to boot. He could do this.

It fell into one of his games. Up over the flat-top rock. Slide underneath the fallen tree. He laughed when he heard the thud of one of the goblins hitting its head underneath the tree. They had to go under just right, or it wouldn't be pleasant.

A dagger whistled past his ear, and buried itself in the tree next to him. He skidded to a stop, and raised his hand to his cheek. When he pulled his fingers back they were spotted with blood.

Careful. He could hear Professor Metteus chiding him. *This is quite real. And like you said, the danger has to be real.*

Oh, no. It was getting harder to breathe, to see. It couldn't be real, this wasn't real, it was just supposed to be a game, a story.

Bree tripped over a tree root. He went sprawling, head over heels into the earth. No, no, the goblins would get him. They'd tear him apart. They'd...*focus. What do you need?*

Bree needed help. He needed a friend right now. Like Kelly, she was always there to keep him out of a scrape. She would know what to do now.

Something tapped Bree on the top of his head. He looked up, and tried not to stare. A rope dangled in front of his face.

"Come on, Bree!" A voice shouted from above. "Grab on!"

Bree grasped the rope, and Kelly jumped out of the tree. The goblins broke through the trees as Bree sailed up to the branches above.

Bree looked on as Kelly...no, Keira, threw herself at the five goblins. Armed with a curved short sword, it danced against the clumsy dagger strikes. The finer steel clanged against the iron. One of the daggers shattered in its master's grasp, leaving the goblin with only a hilt and a hope.

Who is your friend?

That was Keira. Funny, daring Keira. Her hair today was like black fire, jutting up in flames kept close to her scalp. Her golden eyes glinted against her auburn skin. Even in the heat of battle, there was a grin on her face.

Bree caught himself staring. But how could he not? Keira was wearing one of her favorite outfits. Black pants, and a leather tunic that left her arms bare to the shoulder. For movement, and because she liked the salt air on her skin. Bree didn't complain. *Is this a love story?* No! No, this was an adventure. Keira was a friend, a mate. Not that kind. Bree was blushing, he hoped Keira couldn't see.

"Quit staring like an idiot and get down here!" Keira shouted up at him. "I'm enjoying the fun, but some help could...oh, dang it!" She parried a dagger, spun the sword in her grip, and punched at a goblin that got too close.

"Just move!"

Bree jumped out of the tree. Keira pushed a goblin towards him, and Bree landed on the monster's head. The two crumbled to the ground, and Bree emerged victorious. He thrust out with his staff, catching a goblin in the back before it got too close to Keira. It yelped, and fell. Keira slammed her foot down on the beast's head.

The two spun back to back, ready to meet any other foe. But the goblins had had enough, and melted into the forest.

Keira laughed, and hugged Bree. "That was fun!"

She smacked him over the head. "But you were supposed to meet me at the inn. When I heard you left early I had to look everywhere for you."

Bree shrugged, and kept trying to find a reason to blink. Keira was quite a few inches taller than him, and since she turned fifteen she was developing some interesting...mate! Wrong word, no, that was the wrong word. Friend, buddy, pal, platonic.

Besides, she was fifteen. Best to put it out of his head, and focus on the fun things. Like...what were they going to do again?

"You forgot already?" Keira rolled her eyes. "Typical, Bree. We're supposed to get to the titan's lair by nightfall, and you're down in the valley playing with goblins."

Right! The titan's lair. Bree saw it now. A giant had plagued the villages around Greenshere for weeks now. A terrible thing that had torn through the countryside with reckless abandon. Its lair was found settled in the southern mountains. And they were supposed to get to it this evening, how could he have forgotten?

Nor could he forget the giant's master. Prometheus, the crazed Titan. He sat above the giant's castle, pulling the strings from above. Prometheus would not be denied.

Keira cleaned her sword and started south. "Come on. We have to figure out how to beat the giant before we get there."

We don't know? How could they possibly not know how to beat the giant?

Keira glared at Bree. "Because we're twelve and fifteen, Bree. Geez, pay attention. And keep up!"

That was the end of that. The boy Bree started asking questions, every sort of question. Can the giant be felled by mortal weapons? Keira didn't know. How about a mortal weakness? Not a clue. What kind of minions did the creature have? The girl was within seconds of smacking Bree over the head.

He'd wait for a few seconds. Ponder whether or not now was a good time to ask another question. Bree would decide against it, wait again, and then ask the question. Keira flipped between answering with an "I don't know," or chasing Bree up a nearby fir. Soon enough the sun started to dip from the sky.

"We have no clue about what we're doing," Bree commented.

"Doesn't matter," Keira said. "We'll figure it out when we get there."

"How?"

That seemed dangerously close to one of his annoying questions. Bree shifted his weight towards an oak tree, to avoid so many needles. Instead, Keira's shoulders slumped.

"We need to do this, Bree. No matter how, it needs to be done."

"I know that," Bree scuffed his shoe. He wasn't stupid. And yet here he was, fighting a giant of Prometheus', with no clue of how to beat it. But on they went. Towards the castle lair.

Bree led, past the trees and comforts of Anworth forest. *You are making a wonderful mistake.* A mistake? Perhaps, perhaps it was at that. Bree knew that he might be risking his life. Certainly the tales told in Greenshere about any who ventured near the Chained One never ended happily. But the giant had stood up to the best the lands had to offer. Bree was willing to ask for help.

He and Keira came into view, clearing a last copse of trees, and hung back. The chains lay before them. Iron links, each as big around as Bree's torso. They were bound together, and driven into the rocks by iron spikes. Four such chains were clasped to enormous wrists and ankles, and there he was. The Chained One.

The Chained One, you may ask? For he was known, certainly. Bree and Keira could tell all the tales of him. He had broken the rules, defied authority. For this he had been chained to the rocks, forced to live out eternity in agony.

He was twenty feet tall, strapped to the side of the mountain. He was naked save for a cloth garment covering his waist to his knees. His arms and legs struggled and writhed against the stone. It was unclear which would break first. His chest was that of an Adonis, finely chiseled against the granite behind him - save for the gaping wound in his abdomen. It bled freely, and continued to do so as Keira and Bree considered their next move.

As for his face, he looked...he looked like professor Metteus. The eyes were the same shade of green oak leaf, the curled hair was just as rich. But there the sameness ended. The hair was plastered to the Chained One's face where Metteus would have it meticulous. And his eyes darted about the landscape, bloodshot and teary. He could not fixate upon a single object for longer than a glance.

"Children of Greenshere," He murmured. His words were crackling fire, and used sparingly. "Come closer."

Discovered, Keira and Bree picked their way towards the behemoth. They stayed on one side of the chains, just out of reach. The two remained silent, and stared at the man.

"Do you mock me?" he laughed. It rumbled through the hills and their ears. "Have I sunk so low in this rock that even children are above my station?"

"You deserve it!" Keira shouted. She gasped, and clasped her hand to her mouth before it could speak again.

"Deserve it?" The titan stopped laughing. "What was my crime? What did I do that merited such torment?"

"You offended the gods."

"I saved humanity!" The titan thundered.

Bree had a passing thought. A memory from another self, floating through the ether. He reached up, caught it, and let it go.

"Prometheus?"

"The name is so," The titan muttered. "I, chained for compassion that was wasted on such a lowly race. I languish in torment because I risked all to give you humans the gift of fire.

Knowledge was my gift! And you have all forgotten it because the gods deemed it so."

Keira turned around. She stood, and shifted on her toes. She balanced on one leg, and then the other. She scrunched her eyes tight, then opened them as wide as possible before breathing. She turned back around.

"So you say..." She began.

This was not right. Prometheus was not the Chained One. He was the hidden master, the ruler of monsters. Crouching from on high, ready to do...something. That last part was always glossed over.

"You know it to be true." Prometheus said. "Think on my tale. Remember."

They did remember. The tale was old, older than Greenshere itself, but it was real. A tale of gods, wrapped up in petty squabbles and vanity. Divine beings that took away fire rather than share it with humans who had to scratch their way through the dirt. The world grew cold, and dark, and bleak. Humans huddled together for warmth, and still died out slowly.

Then the titan Prometheus stole fire from its hiding place. With honeyed words and guile he slipped past the defenses of the gods. He hid fire within a hollowed stick, and bestowed it to humanity. For his insolence the gods bound him in iron, strung him upon a rock, and set a bird to tear into his flesh and devour his liver. His wound would heal every day so that he could be tormented again the next morning. This was Prometheus' punishment for aiding man.

Keira and Bree could feel the fog of memory fade as the true tale settled in their minds. It seemed ridiculous to even consider the false tale had once prevailed as factual. Keira slammed her sword against the chains. Iron was met with steel, and the steel clanged away without leaving a dent.

"Save your strength, woman," Prometheus said.

"Not happening," Keira muttered. "We're going to rescue you, and then we'll beat the giant together, and the day will be saved."

"Saved?"

"From the giant," Keira swung her sword against the chain again. The blade rang out again, and Keira almost dropped it. That clang, it knocked a memory loose! The giant did not protect Prometheus, but rather kept him in chains. That had to be stopped!

"Ah," Prometheus looked on. "I know the giant. You will not last long against him."

"That's why we are going to need your help."

Prometheus nodded. "Then I would hurry."

Keira gritted her teeth. "That's what I'm doing."

"Because the giant sent his minions."

The giant's minions! The ghouls, the goblins. The snargles and rasks that shuddered out of the hills in the waning light to find the two children who dared trespass on their mountain. Nightmares stampeded before them, whinnying with dreams and terrors in their wake.

Keira clutched her sword close, and leapt towards the enemy. "Bree, free Prometheus!"

Bree held his stick close, and looked at the girl as she vaulted over a nightmare. "How?"

Keira grunted, and sliced her sword. She parried an ill-timed blade, and ran a vapish through. "I don't know! Be clever!"

Be clever. Be clever. Bree beat the stick against the chains a few times. No, that was stupid, come on! Think about what freeing Prometheus would truly mean. He is a titan, a being of enormity and wondrous feats. Shaking a material at his confinement would do little. It must be something more, something elemental.

The boy's eyes widened. He set the stick next to the iron. Picking up two links, he scraped the rusted metal together. It screeched in Bree's ears, promising more pain if he held on.

Bree instead redoubled his efforts, and kept rubbing the metal. A spark flew off the chain, landing with malice on his foot. Bree grimaced, and held on. Keira spun around, holding on to her sword for dear life. Were she to drop it for an instant, or stop and glance back at her friend, she surely would be dashed to pieces. She trusted in him, and continued on. Bree smashed the links together, and a rush of flashes spurted out towards the ground. The grass blackened and singed, and the stick started to smoke.

Once more, Bree. Strike the chain once more, and let the strike be true. He slammed the chain against itself. Iron shards blew apart, fire lighting on the stick and setting it ablaze.

Bree snatched up the torch, and held it aloft towards the titan.

"Grab it!" He shouted.

Prometheus shook his head. "Child, what would a stick do?"

"Come on, the giant can't be far behind his minions," Bree pleaded. "Grab the torch, and help us fight."

Prometheus looked down. "I cannot. I am bound."

"Yes, but you can change that!" Bree shouted. "You are the Titan of fire and knowledge. You looked at a world that cowered in darkness, and risked everything to give it light. If you can't do something with a fire-stick...of course you can, damn you! You're Prometheus."

Prometheus frowned.

"Dammit, Prometheus!" Brian screamed. "Wake up!"

The giant appeared. The giant had come! A bulbous creature, hulked over its bulging torso. It shambled forth, stumbling over its own creatures. It snarled and drooled, snapping at those who got in its way. It pointed a long, diseased claw at the children, before looking away towards some unseen enemy.

The giant let out a lowing cry, and charged.

Prometheus strained once, and grasped the torch by the flame. It flared once, and almost seemed to catch and grow in his grip. If the fire scorched his flesh, he did not give a sound. He adjusted his grip, and thrust the blaze into his chains. The iron gave a screech of protest, before all four burst apart.

He landed to the turf. His wound had healed, disappeared. Prometheus held the torch high, and glared straight ahead. He held his focus on the giant, and his face was contorted in full fury.

"Bree," Prometheus murmured. He looked down at the boy, and his eyes were filled with sorrow. "I apologize."

Bree almost asked why. But Prometheus raised a hand for silence. "This is supposed to be a tale of wonder. Of great joy and triumph for youth. But this is my story, and I used you. This is my burden to set aside, and I thank you for lighting my way."

Bree didn't quite understand.

Prometheus stared at the giant. It had slowed, and howled once. Prometheus' eyes narrowed, and he pointed his torch at the beast.

"I name thee, Ignorance! Foul beast, what right do you have to arrogance, to might? Go back to the depths, and cower there with your small terrors."

Prometheus thrust the torch forward. It flared greater, brighter than the sun.

"I cast you out!"

The torch was white now. White light that burned Bree's eyes. He held them shut in his hands, and still white bled through.

"I cast you out!"

There was nothing but white. There was never anything but white. White light is all colors, blended together in a rush of truth too blinding to behold. Bree couldn't see. He couldn't hear. He couldn't breathe.

"I cast you out!"

Brian shrugged. "At least, that's how I would tell the story."

Professor Metteus frowned. He leaned against the desk, his cane all but forgotten in the desk chair. His fingers tapped against the hardwood, almost waiting for a different ending.

Kelly was seated next to the door. She had completely forgotten when she had entered. It had been important at the time, almost urgent to get Brian's attention. Now she had to blink and remind herself what her name was, let alone where this body was rooted to.

Brian for his part was standing on a chair. His arms stretched wide in accepting the glory of the light, head thrust back and eyes closed. This was life, this was truth. There was an ultimate, and he had found it.

"Hey, dummy," Kelly muttered. "You're going to make me late."

Brian opened an eye. He raised a foot, and looked at it. Perhaps it had changed during his story. Had it, and he hadn't noticed? And changed back? He didn't know if he could trust his foot.

The young man set his foot on the floor, and leaned on it. The appendage didn't give way. Perhaps it was okay to trust it. For now.

Professor Metteus straightened, and nodded. "That is a good tale. Not magnificent, but serviceable."

Serviceable? Brian looked at his teacher. "What just happened?"

"A wakening," The teacher stretched, and nodded. "A passionate one, to be sure."

Brian grinned, sheepish. He had completely forgotten what day it was. "Sorry, I guess I got a little involved in the tale. It almost seemed real."

Metteus cocked his head to one side. "It wasn't?"

The professor gathered his bag, and smiled. "It was felt in the mind, seen through the heart. The tale was spoken, and came alive in ways that defied expectation. Who cares if the reality of this world disagrees with such a story?"

"What does Prometheus want to do?" Kelly asked.

"I imagine he would want to stretch his legs," Professor Metteus said. "As do we all. The world is so dark, so heavy, that we often get lost in its weight. Even a Titan can become discouraged, to the point of preferring chains to action."

He walked towards the door, and the smile had become a grin. "But this is just one version of life. We make our own reality in every breath. Every moment a spark that can catch a new light."

Metteus strode out.

Kelly and Brian glanced at each other.

"Couldn't be." Kelly began.

"You think?"

"For some reason, Professor Metteus left his cane," Kelly said.

The two looked at each other, then bolted for the door. They looked down each hallway, straining to catch a glimpse of a tweed jacket or a spindly titan.

Instead, all they could gather was a smell of smoke in the air. When they returned to the room the cane was still there.

Brian picked it up, and almost dropped the wood. It was still hot, scorched black at the handle. Soot covered Brian's hand. He didn't know whether to stare at the cane or his hand.

Kelly walked next to Brian as they left the school. The day was still bright, the sun just beginning its dip towards the ground. Around them the trees rustled an invitation, while the road beckoned to be walked.

The girl nudged her friend. "Hey,"

"What?"

Kelly pointed to the trees. "Let's go find an adventure."

Brian smiled. "Where?"

Keira smirked.

"Wherever we want."

Cheating Spells

He didn't mean to upset his Spell. He just wanted a piece of pie.

No, he thought, *not just a piece of pie.* This was a magnificent pie, a pie that bards would not dare to sing of. How could their mere voices compare to the taste, the smell, the sensation of that concoction gliding down the throat in jubilation? There would be no songs of this pie, they would not be enough. No, instead, there would be pie.

The Spell. Think of your poor Spell. He brushed the thoughts from his mind.

He really, really wanted pie.

It was a new Charm. A conjuring that he had found in a gastro-alchemical cookbook. Chance encounter, something he hadn't even considered. It was not his, but after he had read the words he didn't care, he was going to *make* it his.

Just the text, just mere words on the page made his mouth salivate. This pie was flamed with magma conjured down from the finest heavens, brought to bear that he could experience such sweet succulence.

And the delectable ingredients, he could barely consider the tastes laid before him. *Apples,* he thought, *apples and red currant.* The apples were brought forth from his own imagination, the currants not. No one truly remembered or imagined a best way for currants to be, chance it had to be plucked out of the ether of currant ideal. Spiced with a dash of alchemy, the fruits melding to cinnamon and liquid life. *What did liquid life taste like?* He asked this of himself, but the Charm just assured him it would be delicious. *She was calm, reassuring,* he thought. *She understood.*

That was it. He had to have this pie. He gripped his wand carefully, and spoke the words. Spoke them trippingly, with just the right lilt to barely contain his excitement.

The wind tore his clothes open. He was revealed, exposed, and the Charm fled him. Back into the book where she belonged, and it slammed shut and locked the cover. It understood the bonds, broken and violated. It understood fear.

His Spell had arrived. In fury she rose out of nothing to appear before him. *Cheater,* she whispered.

He was soon being force fed these words by the Spell. A quaint thing, a memory really, not more than that. It was a recipe for an old flame of his, he wasn't seeing other spells. The pie had nothing to do with how he felt about the cake. Her cake.

Cake was amazing, it had its place, and cheesecake truly was a marvel in dairy confection, she protested.

Both he and the Spell knew he was lying. How could he go back to bone-dry powder when this succulent Charm lay on the tongue? One simply was better, and she just couldn't measure up to this new Charm's pie.

He spoke the words of his Spell again, pleading with it. The diction flowed from his tongue, and he felt ashamed. There was a better way to approach breaking up with a piece of magic.

The Spell, for its part, tried its best not to tear him apart across ethereal winds. It wasn't usually so close to being alive, but magic was a tricky thing. It chose when it would be alive, or was it that it was chosen to be alive? Magic is a confection that does not know its own recipe.

But the Spell did know it was angry. *How could he?* Had this Spell not given him everything he had ever asked for? There had never been a cake that was not provided. Even those rum-soaked things that left him crawling on the floor for the next two days. The Spell was betrayed.

No, that was not true. There had been fault both ways. That last carrot cake had had a rabbit attached, armed with buck teeth and buckshot. And the pound cake had almost flattened him, the poor thing. It was time for a break.

The Spell and her caster looked at each other with lost longing. He had always liked the way the Spell had tasted on the tongue, when it sailed through the winds. And he wasn't so bad, just needed to floss before he tried the hard consonants. The sorrow was true and shared.

Still, he cheated on the Spell. If she just let this stand, where would she be? *What would I be?*

So the mage was bound in a pie tin for one hundred years. Perhaps less if the spell was feeling generous. *He was cute, and often nice. Maybe sooner, if he wanted a piece of cake.*

Mars: Year 1

"Control Center Ares! Come in Ares!"

The crew of Daedalus turned towards the transmission. Earth wasn't supposed to reach out until 0900 for an update. And that wasn't their contact on the ground.

Commander Newman went towards the receiver. Maybe they left enough time to send a response.

"Control Center Ares, do not attempt to respond. There isn't enough time."

Sathi looked up. Past the base, towards the ship Daedalus. What was going on on Earth?

"At present, Earth is engaged in a nuclear holocaust. We don't know if it's the Russians, or China, maybe religious extremists...dammit, I don't know!

"I don't have enough time, but NASA command, what's left of it, is reaching out to all our missions currently off world. *Stay there.* I repeat, do not come back to Earth."

Don't come back? The crew of the Daedalus was six months into a two-year mission. Don't try to come back now? Ever?

"We cannot guarantee either a secure landing site, or even if this planet will be habitable in time for a nine-month mission." The woman a million miles away was fighting back tears. The crew could only listen in.

"Your new parameters are this. Moon base *Bifrost* is currently stable, but they are preparing to launch towards you with drone ships carrying all viable material. The ship *Icarus* is already en-route towards your position, giving the Ares base an expected crew of forty-seven, far surpassing the resources we have sent to Mars. Especially given the lack of a return date.

"You will hold at Ares, expand if need be. When life is no longer sustainable, return with whoever remains."

Silence cut over the transmission. Phoebe grabbed the receiver. "This is Daedalus! What can we do? Please let us... "

"Officer," Commander Newman said. She pulled Phoebe back. "Let us hear."

"I am so sorry the world ended without you," The contact said. "My name is Marcia Dolethal. I'm the receptionist. Everyone is trying to not die, and we might have to let you starve to save you from a poisoned planet. At least you are spared the apocalypse.

"Dear father in heaven, please bless all..."

The Daedalus mission listened in. There was no expansion, no further instructions. Static buzzed through the compound.

"What happened?" Colin asked. There had to be an explanation. What was going to happen next?

Commander Newman knew better. It took seven minutes for a transmission from Earth to reach Mars. The signal travelled across space, regardless of what happened back at the origin. Regardless of the situation, even a receptionist would follow protocol and end the transmission correctly, if she could.

For all intents and purposes, Earth ended ten minutes ago.

Mars being safer for the astronauts. To the point of risking the crew of the Daedalus' lives with the intake of two more teams. Dr. Wendy Fenix couldn't believe it.

She was where she was safe, in her lab. This place made sense. A series of equations that added up to life, death, transformation, anything rational. Not a nuclear holocaust, not utter loss, and dammit why? Why did they have to go and do it?

Wendy sat at her desk, and wept. No going back home. Stuck in this cold dust across the stars. Her friends were most likely dead or dying. She was stuck here. With them.

The chemist cried for five minutes. She allowed herself that, before she opened a notebook. She called for the Commander, and started to study her notes.

"Commander, I've been running the data and...well..."

"We are screwed." Commander Newman examined the vials. She had a doctorate from MIT, five years of flight experience, and a medal from the president for her work developing the Daedalus site. A medal that was most likely radioactive, next to the degree in astronautics. All told, fifteen years of higher education. And the Commander still didn't understand some of the contents in this lab. She had just signed on the dotted line for authorization.

"Is there a miracle in one of these?"

Fenix shrugged. "Maybe. Wish I could say. Haven't had a chance to examine the soil samples."

"Not in the mood for wishes, Wendy," Newman muttered. "I need facts, not platitudes."

"Facts?" Wendy pointed back towards earth. "The only source of sustainable life is glowing green right now. We're about to *quadruple* the capacity of this station, with barely enough supplies as it is. I'd give us maybe six months before the *Icarus* lands, another four and *Bifrost* stumbles in. Then we ration, and die by inches."

"You are not in charge of rations, Dr." Trisha Newman sighed. "You and Dee Leif are in charge of one thing, and one thing only. Make Mars grow."

"Really?" The chemist laughed. She clutched her sides and rolled to the ground. This was insanity. Wendy Fenix didn't laugh, she barely chuckled. For her entire life the chemist had controlled everything about her body. Didn't feel too happy, or sad, or high, and all without medicinal help. Now she had just spent the last five minutes buffeted upon a sea of emotions that was relentless.

It was actually rather refreshing.

Trisha watched her chemist fight her way through feelings. She felt a twinge of happiness, but it was mostly because she had bet Sathi that Fenix was going to be the first to crack. She had just won three dollars.

"Thank you, Commander," Wendy stood up. "I'm going to find Dee. After this we're going to solve peace in the Middle East."

Commander Newman looked up toward the sky. "That might be easy now, all things considered."

Dee was dressed like Matt Damon, as usual. It was understandable, kind of. The movie was eighteen years old, seemingly accurate, and the botanist wanted to emulate that damn movie in all its aspects. She even had that orange space suit tailor made, complete with a fake crack in the helmet.

She was Scandinavian. And a botanist. And Wiccan. And blonde. Wendy Fenix was under orders to spend the rest of her life next to this botanist, for the salvation of the crew of three separate missions, and quite possibly the remainder of the human race.

Or she could try and do anything else. Like just wish fresh air to spread across the planet. That might be less painful.

"Where have the boys run off to?" Dee asked. "Marcus, and Colin, and Daavos and Kaaba?"

"Errands of their own." There were men on the crew of *Daedalus*. Truly, and honestly. But this had been a hard-fought victory for Commander Newman, to be able to look her boss in the eye and say with confidence and evidence that the women were overqualified for the mission. The boys, as they were affectionately known by all the women on board, kept to themselves. They were afterthoughts, politically speaking. Chosen because they were too qualified (or connected, as the rumors were for Daavos) to be denied the opportunity.

"A shame," Dee ran her hand across the floor. "Masculine elements would balance our own. We need both in a creation spell."

No. Not this again. Wendy already had to deal with working with Dee for the rest of her life. She was not starting off with Dee's mad obsession with magic.

"It's not madness, Wendy," Dee murmured. "Mars is alive, just sleeping. Magic is sitting there, just beneath the surface. We need to find it."

"No, no no no no no. No." Wendy knelt down and looked at Dee. "What we need is to start brainstorming Dee. Do you know what Commander Newman asked us to do?"

"Create sustainable food. If we manage enough plants, possibly start synthesizing breathable air."

Wendy nodded. "Yes, so we need to start..."

"The creation spell." Dee laid face down on the floor. "I was thinking Kaaba. Someone different might give us some new results."

"Dee, you aren't listening!" Wendy stood up. "We need to figure out a way to start growing..."

"The air is too thin," Dee said. "It may be mostly carbon dioxide, but typical plants couldn't take in enough for photosynthesis. Besides which they would freeze without a heated enclosure. Then there's irrigation. And without a planetary magnetic field, all base extensions will need proper shielding against radiation."

She looked up at Wendy. "Still think the spell is stupid?"

Yes she did. Just because the task given seemed impossible, did not mean we abandoned rational thought. We stuck to facts and formulae, the solid engineering that had proven useful in getting so many people to cross the skies.

Maybe the botanist was just too caught up in her own thing. Dee prayed to nature, the great Earth spirit. A spirit that was on fire, if it ever existed. Maybe it was that, this complete destruction that so broke the woman.

"If it's about CO_2 conversion..." Wendy looked around for a marker. The lab was pristine, even filled with all sorts of soil samples and seeds from Earth. If nothing else, Dee's madness was contained and correlated to a filing system. "If it is about providing enough CO_2, we can pull it from the air. Martian atmosphere *is* 95% carbon dioxide..."

Wendy pointed west, towards the plant that had been sent over a few years ago. "There is an air-filtration system designed to capture and process oxygen from the atmosphere. We can take one of the pumps. A little tweaking, a few lines of code, and it can start collecting the CO_2 for us immediately. Grab a back-up O_2 regulator and make some adjustments, we can add to the greenhouse sustainability."

Dee looked out, and frowned. This was true, and it was possible. The whole reason she was here was to start deliberating

possible scenarios for terraforming Mars. But it was much too soon, too fast, and this wasn't a real solution.

"We don't even have a decent water supply." Dee muttered.

"What are you talking about?" Wendy pointed south. "There's a permafrost deposit half a mile south."

"What?" Dee leaped up. Her designs scattered on the ground, forgotten. "We don't have any surface scans of permafrost near here."

The chemist rolled her eyes. "It's thirty meters below the surface. The scanners shouldn't have picked it up, but it's there."

She set off towards the boys. Seriously, she knew there was water there. She could feel it, just calling to her. Dee could understand gut feelings, right? Or did she need to be told by the sand that it was close by?

"You want me to what?"

Marcus could only be properly described as a dude. His hair hung down to his shoulders in dreads, and most likely held some bit of grease or other byproduct from working in the shop.

Wendy tried to fight a way through to a grin. Marcus was annoyingly chill, and relaxed to a point of half-asleep. But he was the only one who could properly operate Dig-Dug. So she had to respect him, even if it felt like she was getting maimed with a spoon.

"You're going to take the pneumatic drill and dig at coordinates 9.56 and 47.3 degrees south of our position."

"But...why?"

The urge to smack him was strong. Wendy instead sighed, took a deep breath, and showed the calculations.

"There have been thermal scans that show a difference in temperature, and there has been shifts in the geography..."

"Seriously, Wendy," Marcus stared at her. "What the hell are you talking about?"

"Yes, Doctor Fenix," The three turned to see Commander Newman. She leaned against the door to Dig-Dug's garage. The commander did not pleased. In fact, her short-cropped hair bristled at Dee's confused message over the communications system.

"What exactly are you talking about?"

Wendy grimaced. "Well...commander, I was just trying to explain to Marcus that if he took the drill to this new position, I believe that there is a store of permafrost just thirty meters below the surface."

"Believe? On what evidence?" The commander surveyed a nearby desk of Marcus' cluttered notes. "The thermal scans and shifts you described haven't been recorded by anyone else. In fact, they've only shown up in your reports, afterthoughts with barely any notation or proof."

"But they're there!" Wendy stared at a blank wall. She could feel the water, stuck in one place. It was so close, it called out to her.

Called out to her? What was Doctor Fenix thinking? This wasn't rational, this didn't even seem lucid. It was something that Dee would be thinking, calling out to a frozen sea.

"I'm sorry," Wendy looked at the commander. "I must be a little bit out of it."

Newman stared ahead for a while, and tapped Marcus on the head.

"Do a scan."

Marcus shook his head. "Can't. If she's right about the depth, the scanners wouldn't penetrate the soil."

Newman nodded. "All right then. Prep Dig-Dug."

"Come again?"

"Did I ask, technician?"

That was the answer to that. Commander Newman looked to the chemist and botanist, and smiled.

"I believe that you, Dr. Lief, have some dried herbs secreted away for a soothing tea. Perhaps the two of you would be kind enough to join me for a tic whilst Marcus gets Dig-Dug to the coordinates?"

The two doctors had to watch their commander walk away. They stood in stunned silence. Dee nudged Wendy.

"I know."

"But she just did the..."

"I *know*."

"I think I'm in love," Dee muttered.

There was something that had to be understood about the crew of the *Daedalus*. They were from nine countries spread across four continents. Any of nineteen languages could have an immediate translator, including Greek, Mandarin, Hebrew, English, German, Latin and Coptic. There were specialists in everything from electrical engineering to biomedical research, all working in the name of improving life on the red planet. Between the twelve members there was a grand total of one hundred and seventeen years of higher education, and another one hundred and twenty in professional experience in space. They were extremely qualified, beyond fearless, and committed to the goal of exploration and study of Mars.

And each and every one of them could be considered one of the biggest sci-fi nerds back on earth.

This was a quantifiable fact. There were episodes of every *Star Trek* series that ran almost constantly at the Ares base. There were heated debates about DC and Marvel, and which Doctor Who was in fact the best. The crew even had a running pool on which famous space captain Commander Newman secretly compared herself to.

Seeing her lounged in a chair, a steaming cup of tea in one hand, made the chemist and botanist reassess what their selections were.

"Wonderful. And aged, which is all we can receive at the moment," the commander took another sip. Just a hint of spice, glorious.

"Thank you, Commander." Dee shuffled in her seat.

"A shame that it may be one of the last cups left." Trisha said sadly. She shook her head, and cradled the cup. "We are ending an era."

The girls nodded.

"So why do you think Marcus is going to hit permafrost in the next fifteen minutes?"

"That's a little hard to explain," Wendy began.

"Well, I have read your reports," Trisha pointed to a stack of files. "I was just reviewing them, and just as I thought. A little side note once or twice a week about the possibility of a site near our location, though never before with such accuracy.

"You seem convinced that there is water within reach. It was just an afterthought, not truly important enough, and you never called for an exploration on your hypothesis."

"No, commander."

"Why is that?"

Wendy shook her head. "I didn't mean that I never called for exploration commander. It's not a hypothesis."

Trisha arched an eyebrow. "Really?"

Wendy shrugged. "In thirteen minutes, Marcus is going to call you, absolutely flabbergasted and more excited than we have seen him since we launched."

"So you can predict the future?"

"Not really. I'm just guessing about Marcus. But it would make sense."

"That it would."

Wendy frowned. "Could I look at the reports?" There had been so many, almost one every three sols, she did not even remember some of them. With a nod of assent she started poking through the reports.

Sure enough, twelve sols in was her first reference to water being within reach. She couldn't even remember making the note. Again a few days later, and again. Every third or fourth report had some reference to the permafrost that was in easy access to the crew. No wonder she was convinced.

"You see the question." Trisha Newman took her cup towards the soil samples. "I have here a chemist who, if right, just provided a source of water and new materials that could be instrumental in our survival. If wrong, is a little crazy."

"I assure you..." Dr. Fenix trailed off on the latest report in her hand. That wasn't her handwriting. "This is...a soil report from Dr. Lief."

"Right, I've been looking over both of your ideas since you've arrived. Actually, what's amazing is the difference in both of your writings before and after arrival."

It was a remarkable difference. Not in style, but in substance. Trisha was almost in awe of the new character the two doctors had taken on. Both had begun stating facts, practiced theorems with clear references to data and figures. Within weeks the two had kept their references, but they theorized on Mars atmosphere and chemical content with such confidence that they had to be taken as fact. There was water close by the Ares base. A topographic map of the region, with chemical composition already filled in.

"And then there was this one," Trisha Newman held up a report. "There's life on Mars, Dr. Lief?"

Dee cleared her throat. "The *potential* for life, Commander. I think I was quite clear."

"Not enough atmosphere, no arable soil, solar radiation that would fry anything brave enough to step outside without protection. That is your potential?"

"The potential is within Mars itself." Dee countered. A bit harsher than she had wanted. But there she went, straight ahead.

"Commander, the planet has been dead for untold millennia. What was here, why did it die, I have no idea. But the planet is ready *now*. He knows what happened to his sister, he grieves. He wants to help us rebuild. Mars wants to live."

Dee had to be certifiable. This whole Wicca lifestyle was fun and amusing, but she was ignoring science. Wendy almost sighed in disbelief. *She* was ignoring science.

"You're Wiccan, correct?"

"Yes, commander," Dee replied.

"A spiritual connection to the natural world. I remember going through that in undergrad." Trisha turned to Wendy. "Yourself, Dr. Fenix?"

"I don't believe in a god that just let a planet die," Wendy responded.

"True enough, true enough." The Commander took another sip, and smiled. Still hot, not scalding. Perfect. "I myself have never been in a religious organization. Agnostic is the term I suppose, but I've always questioned the word. It's not that I just believed in something unnamed, it just seemed like there was something out there that just had not been properly defined."

She threw the tea in Wendy's face. The chemist gasped, threw her hands up. She felt a surge of energy, a wave that flowed from her core to her fingertips and out.

The tea stopped a foot away from her, and hung in midair.

Dee looked on in awe. "Mother Earth preserve us."

Commander Newman smirked. "Father Mars might be more appropriate, Dr. Lief."

Wendy shook from her head to her toes. Her hands blurred. It appeared to be a stroke, or a heart attack. Anything that was more believable than this.

The commander took an empty bucket, and placed it underneath the tea.

"Just relax, Wendy," Trisha whispered. "Just relax, let it go. Breathe."

She hadn't done that in a while. She gulped a lungful of air. The tea wavered, and burst down, splashing into the container.

"Good tea not gone to waste," The commander said. "Though it served a purpose, regardless."

Wendy stared at her hands. The horror on her face scared her to just consider it.

"This is impossible," She breathed.

Trisha smiled. "I think we're going to have to remove that word for a while."

"Commander? This is Marcus, reporting in."

She tapped the communicator. "Thank you, Marcus. How much permafrost was there?"

"How did you – I honestly don't know. It's way too big for Dig-Dug to take in one go."

"Good to know. Get as big a piece for analysis in Dr. Fenix's lab, then put Dig-Dug to bed. Good work."

"What the hell is going..." Newman cut the transmission before the profanity could get any cruder.

"Ladies, I think it's time to hold a meeting with the full crew."

"So that's what happened," The commander looked across the HAB. While the doctors Fenix and Lief didn't show emotion, the rest of the crew was staring at her openmouthed.

"Permission to speak freely, commander?" Colin asked. As head of security, he still had some military tendencies that had to be broken through.

"Granted."

"Are you off your rocker?"

Newman's eyebrows rose. "I doubt it. You've seen the data that Marcus and Dig-Dug have collected. The video of Dr. Lief's lab and the incident regarding Dr. Fenix."

"That, that was..." Sathi was their astronomer, and flabbergasted. "That was a trick. A gravitational anomaly brought on by the aftershocks felt here after the incidents back on Earth..."

"What Sathi is trying to say is we have no clue what is going on." Commander Newman said.

Dee wanted to speak, but wisely kept her mouth shut. The commander had been very clear about her ideas. As much as she wanted to set up the spells and a functional potions lab, that had to wait. It was hard enough convincing the rest of the crew that she wasn't insane. Wendy still thought she was. Dee knew that.

Dee was wrong. Wendy didn't know what to think. She crouched in the corner of the HAB, just trying to disappear. She could feel eyes glancing her way every few moments. What was happening? Wendy was a doctor of Chemistry. She broke the laws of chemistry, and physics, and the human body.

"Dr. Fenix. Dr. Fenix."

Wendy would have sworn she was insane. But everyone believed her. What did that make her?

"Wendy!"

She looked up. Dee was next to her, nodding. "She's here."

Commander Newman looked at the rest of the crew. "Dr. Fenix. Do you think you can explore these new abilities?"

"Un...under supervision." Wendy whispered. She didn't want to do this alone.

"Always," Trisha pointed to Marcus. "Let's get that ice core inside. I want us to start examining it as a potential water source. Whatever minerals need to be extracted, there should be other uses for them.

"We are stranded on a planet that doesn't seem to like life. Dee says that's different. Let's prove her right."

The commander sighed, and sat on the table. She remained silent for a moment, drinking in the gaze of her crew.

"What I'm suggesting flies in the face of not just every space regulation, but every law of science reaching back to Boyle and Galileo. In some instances, we will willingly disregard what we once took for facts. This is not the standard, or the opening position.

"First and foremost, this is a team of scientists. We will approach this planet with logic, reason and analyses based in fact. This just may also include accepting phenomena that seem impossible. Impossible is no longer a word we use."

"Dee," Trisha turned. The botanist waved. "She will be both developing soil samples, while discovering what is needed to start growing produce. If you have any ideas, no matter how insane they are, send them her way.

"Even more important is what happens around you," Trisha said. "Anything unusual, either around you, or even to you, I want to know. We don't have the luxury of privacy. Mars is giving us new ways to look at life. Let's start listening."

She stood up. "Let's get to work."

Post-Apocalyptic Flooding

Water. Water rushing, bubbling up over the levies and coursing through the streets. Friends running, a patron screamed. Perry ran out of the café and headed towards a fire escape. He grabbed the rusted iron, and scrambled up the ladder. The smell of brine filled his lungs as he raced up the stairs. Up one flight, another, faster. Have to move faster.

This was supposed to be impossible. Salt Lake City was safe, the wars didn't come this far inland. But this wasn't an attack. It was a disaster.

Perry pulled himself up to the roof, and watched the coursing waves crash against the building. He watched as the Great Salt Lake surged out of the north, and sweep into what was once a capital of America. He didn't know if America still existed. He just wanted to serve coffee and go home. Home must be underwater now.

"This is impossible," a man said. Perry looked at the new man, and was struck by how composed he seemed. His blonde hair was mussed, and had a wound on his shoulder that was still bleeding. His shorts were torn, and soaked. Yet, the man just stared ahead at the oncoming flood.

"The lake was supposed to be drying, not surging," The man murmured. Perry walked forward, and the other man finally noticed him.

"Lucard," The man offered.

"Perry."

They looked out. "Think it's going to stop?" Perry asked.

"No," Lucard said. "It might settle, recede. But the lake's establishing new ground. Most of downtown is never breaking the surface again."

He smiled. "It's almost magic, when you think about it."

"How do you..." Perry began, and Lucard laughed.

"I help manage the library," He sighed. "Managed, at least. It's soaked through."

Perry heard a rumble, and looked to the north. A wave was coming towards him and Lucard, at least two stories high. No, that can't be right. It was bigger than the café!

Lucard laid a hand on Perry's shoulder. "Looks like we've got another one coming."

Perry nodded. "Lucard?"

"Yes?"

"We survive this," he smiled. "Want to grab dinner?"

Lucard laughed. "Start swimming then. I don't want to be late."

The wave crashed into the building. It leapt over the walls, surged through and carried the two away. Perry lost his footing, and slammed his head into the brickwork as he tumbled over the southern edge. He started to lose consciousness as he slipped into the saltwater.

No, that's not right. Perry thought. *The lake just splashed our feet. Lucard and I couldn't stop laughing as we watched the waters recede.*

He started to sink to the road, and could see Lucard fall down next to him.

No, no. Not Lucard...not my darling...

Perry awoke with a gasp. He sat straight up in bed, and shivered. He was covered in sweat, and the cold mountain air only made him shiver and break out in gooseflesh.

Lucard grumbled next to him, and grabbed at the covers. "Not now, Perry. Few more minutes." He garbled it through a pillow before rolling over in bed.

Perry looked back at his husband, and sighed. A dream, it was only a dream.

He stretched, and wiped the sleep from his eyes. He poked Lucard to get him going, and slipped into a long shirt. Perry couldn't wait to get out and see the day in Freedom.

Freedom was set deep in the Rockies. Deep, past any town that had once been worth mentioning. An old mining village that had run dry before the twentieth century, it was perfect for refugees from the former states. While there was no more gold found in the old mine, there was farmland, a clear running river, and enough homes to suit the town of three hundred.

Perry always thought the place was the definition of pastoral. Sitting right on the floor of a valley, he could look at the giant mountains of stone and forest around him, and it gave him comfort. Still did as he walked through the town. There was no war running through here, and too remote to be worth anything to the scattered new states that tried to cobble something after what he and Lucard secretly called the apocalypse.

Perry dipped a hand into the river and splashed some water on his face. He even loved this river. This clear waterway was glacier runoff, the cleanest to be found for miles. There was fish to be found all across, and one of Perry's main jobs was to keep the town stocked with salmon. So far he had been keeping up with the quota.

"Perry! Perry!"

His ears perked up as a little Spanish girl ran up. Calla, she had to have just turned eight. Her bright eyes were perked up at the sight of the man, and she ran screaming towards him.

"Uncle Cluny needs help with the roof!" She shouted. "Hurry and I get a cookie!"

Good old Cluny. Knew exactly how to get the local kids dashing across town as messengers with a hint of a sweet. A former sous chef, the grizzled old Frenchman could cook anything. And probably whip Perry bloody with that sharp tongue of his if he didn't hurry up to the house. Perry picked up the pace, and tried to keep up with Calla as she turned back.

Cluny sat on the edge of a thatch roof, and scowled down as Perry ran up the path. "Monsieur, you are late!"

"Just got the message, you frog," Perry shot back. Late, Perry was always late to Cluny. He was late getting the door installed, or laying the bricks for the chimney. Cluny never told Perry about the little jobs he needed done for his house. That way, the Frenchman could always claim the former waiter was late.

"Your back not holding up against that ego?"

"Bah!" Cluny spat on the ground. "American men, thinks the world waits for none but them. This roof needs to be secured before winter, n'est-ce pas?"

"Oui, oui," Perry said. He scrambled up onto the roof and started spreading thatch. Cluny started barking directions, and pointing just where was lacking a proper layer. Perry felt like he was back at the café. Strangely, the yelling had gotten better with time.

"You missed a spot!" Perry smiled. Missed a spot, missed a drink refill, you didn't smile enough, all the little tirades he had railed against back in Salt Lake. Now, it just seemed comfortable. Perry knew he didn't have a direction, didn't even have one today besides fishing. Cluny was always kind enough to provide a little direction.

Perry almost laughed. Or maybe he was just an ornery cook who knew free help when it walked along. Either was extremely like.

Calla poked her head up on the roof. "Uncle Cluny? Do you have that cookie?"

"Of course, Calla," Cluny muttered. "Just run into the kitchen, and take them out of the oven with your bare hands. Then when your hands are burning, be sure to lower them into the river slowly. Elsewise they might get burned against the rocks."

"Okay!" She said.

Cluny groaned. "I meant, little girl…"

"Relax, Cluny," Perry said. "She's just messing with you." Calla wasn't going to risk ruining that cookie. Such a treat was becoming more and more rare, and even at eight the girl could recognize a treasure that needed to be savored. Even if Cluny might make them more than he should.

Maybe that's why Perry always stopped to help the old cook. Cluny spoiled the town, and they knew it. Where people like Perry made sure the buildings stayed up, there was food on the table, and Cluny gave such food zest, a little joy. Up in the mountains, secluded as they were, that was living in full. A little thatch spreading was worth *joie de vivre*, to steal the French.

"Americans," The chef muttered.

"No one's American." Perry said. "Not anymore. We're all free."

Perry sat on the edge of the roof. He placed his hand down on the thatch, and pressed down. It held firm, good. That should keep the rain out, and the heat in. Cluny was getting a very fine abode, if Perry thought so himself. "You and that little hubby down there," Cluny smirked. "He is very good, no?"

"Absolument," Perry remarked.

"Let him know I'd like a real kitchen?" Cluny pressed. "Cutting board, running water, a full oven, and even some casks for le ferment? I can make it a tavern for the ages."

"A tavern for the ages?" Perry asked. "And who is going there?"

"Nous sommes inviter!" Cluny sometimes lost his English when he was excited. "Who can cook better than I? Let the others farm the fields, and you give me some of those fine fish. I will work wonders for that pretty little mouth."

Perry started laughing, and hopped off the roof. "I'll pass along the request for a masterpiece, Cluny."

"And hurry!" Cluny shouted after the boy. "Greatness must be cultivated!"

Right. And the town had the man hours to give Cluny a full kitchen, and a tavern, and maybe a brewery. Perry hoped the cook was planning this out over a number of years, because there was still plenty that needed to be done now. His wasn't the only thatch roof that needed to be spread, and there were walls that needed to be repaired, and irrigation, and everything that Lucard was saying that Perry would really like to say he completely understood.

Cluny might just have to wait a year. Or two.

Calla jogged up to Perry, fishing poles in hand. "Are we going up to the wall, Perry?"

Perry stopped, and stared at the girl. When had she left? There was chocolate smeared all about her face, and that must have been it. He had told Calla yesterday he was planning on going fishing. She must have had the poles ready at daybreak, just waiting for Perry to wake up and get moving.

But if she had been waiting so long, something must be missing from her day. "We?" Perry looked down at Calla. "Are you done with your chores?"

Lucard walked up. "No, she isn't."

Perry's husband looked down at Calla. "Calla, your mother is looking for you about a cow that is very distraught. Seems it has too much milk."

"But Perry said…"

"I said nothing of the kind," Perry chided her. He picked up the fishing poles out of her hand. "Now quit pitting the couple against itself, you know that won't work."

Calla huffed. "Fine, I'll go do my chores."

Lucard kneeled down, and laid a hand on Calla's shoulder. "Now, look here, young lady." Calla turned away, and Lucard's brow furrowed. "Look at me when I'm talking to you."

Oh, that tone of voice. Perry smiled. Lucard had used it on him once or twice, and knew it would be cruel, kind, and effective. He leaned in closer to listen.

Calla glanced in Lucard's direction. "You are going to milk that cow or else she will start feeling sick, and sweep that front porch like you promised you would do this morning. And then you will put off taking the clothes in, something *else* you promised your mother, on account of them being in need of another few hours on the line. Then, and only then, will Perry take you up to the wall for too much tomfoolery and raucous behavior."

Lucard's eyes glinted with mischief. "Do we understand each other?"

Calla hugged Lucard close, and dashed off to her chores.

Lucard stood up. "You stole the covers all night," He muttered, not looking at Perry so his husband couldn't see the smirk on his face. "Tonight, vengeance shall be mine."

"I look forward to the battle," Perry said. "Which way are you going?"

"Towards the mine," Lucard said. "It's today."

Perry's slumped shoulders didn't escape notice. "We've been over this."

They had. At least six times. Perry could count them off. Fight one was amusing, number two started to grate on his nerves, fight three was just mean until Lucard tripped in his rant and spilled red currant all down his front. That had made fights four and five social, if not agreeable.

Lucard and many of the men were convinced there was good work to be found in the mine. Not gold, no. not coal or anything like that. But good, solid stone that could be used to reinforce the homes. Maybe even a vein of copper. There was so much potential to be found under the earth.

Perry thought it was nice to dream, as long as it wasn't foolhardy. There were crops that could be sown, fish that could be caught now. Buildings that could be rebuilt now. Why risk another cold winter looking for treasure when homes could be made secure?

But Lucard wasn't alone. And he didn't just represent himself. He was the leader of Freedom, mayor in all but name. If men and women were going to risk the mines, then he had to be there in support as well.

Perry was being silly. All would be well.

Lucard patted him on the shoulder. "We'll be back before dusk. Sorry, but you're stuck with cooking tonight."

"Liar," Perry muttered. "I knew you planned this around our cooking schedule."

Lucard laughed, and gave him a kiss before setting off. And a second, to linger on the lips.

"Just because," He said. "Wouldn't want you to forget."

With a wink he was off, and Perry was alone.

He missed Lucard already. Freedom was a bit too lonely at times, especially when Perry was the only one without a specific skill. He had to flit from job to job, always helping, never leading. Lucard had to be in charge, was built for it. Perry just wasn't.

He walked over to the riverbank, and waited. Sure enough, before too long Calla was racing towards him, pigtails flying every which way.

"I'm done!" She declared, and set her hands on her hips to make the declaration even more so. Perry almost burst out laughing, and tussled her hair.

"So you are." He probably should check anyways. At least keep an eye out for Calla's mother in case she came streaking towards them in ire over the slapdash performances.

Calla gave another toothy grin, and Perry relented. Too much cuteness to be denied, damn it all.

Calla looped an arm in Perry's as they walked along.

"Tell me a story, Perry," She pressed.

"A story? And what story would that be?"

"Magic!" Calla shouted.

"Magic?" Perry thought about it for a while. "Okay, once upon a time…"

"Not a 'once upon a time' made-up tale," Calla said. "I want a real magic tale."

Perry's brow furrowed. A real magic tale?

Oh, dear. "You've been listening to travelers and their little stories again."

"Have not!" Calla said. "And besides, they're not just stories."

"Uh hunh." Perry wasn't convinced. He, too, had heard everything. Travelers, either refugees moving west or east in some grand escape, had some tale or other to say. They almost inevitably involved some miracle tale. Flying creatures sailing above the mountains, fairies hiding in clover fields…the dead rising again. It was all to be expected.

Many in Freedom believed that they were living in the end days. Or worse, that the end days had come and gone, and this was all that was left. If that were the case, Perry thought, then let us have our little lives.

"Magic is real," Calla said. "I've seen it!"

"Where?" *Damn it*, Perry thought. *That came out far too harsh.* Perry loosened from Calla, and knelt down next to her. "I mean, where did you see the magic, Calla?"

"The bombs missed us!" Calla said. "Me and mama were right outside L.A. and somehow we ran and dodged all of them."

This was going to be difficult. He didn't want to hurt her, but believing in nonsense was only going to get her hurt, or worse. "Calla, darling, I think that was just luck. Remarkable, incredible, miraculous luck or good fortune. But not magic."

"It was so!" Calla insisted. "It was magic then, and even more when I saw an angel last week."

Perry winced, and got up and continued walking towards the stream. That conversation. Just a few days ago, what was he doing? Skipping rocks, after chopping down a tree that was getting a little too close to one of the main buildings. Get rid of a hazard, and firewood to boot.

Lucard was there, and that was right after fight number…four about the mine. They had made up behind the town hall, and Lucard had had a moment to breathe, so he sat there by the river, and just watched Perry skip rocks across the water.

Then Calla was running again, screaming about some angel in the woods.

"An angel?"

"Does he like salmon?" Lucard said.

"She," Calla said. "Angels can be girls too, you know."

"And what color were her wings?" There was just no changing her mind. Fine, she'll tell her story, and Perry would catch some salmon when he went fishing later. By that night she'd forgotten everything. Or so he had hoped.

Today, she was repeating her story, and once again the details were a little different.

"Gray, and she was looking straight at me," Last week they were blue, and she was looking towards Freedom. Calla jumped up onto the rocks, and looked into the river. "Are we going to catch a bunch of fish?"

"Of course," Perry said. "We've got you as bait."

Calla stuck her tongue out at him. "She was looking straight at me, and then flew away."

"Why?"

"I dunno." Calla said. "I think she was surprised to see me."

She slipped, and fell into the river. "Perry!"

Perry dropped the poles and reached in. calla grabbed his hand, and slipped once before scrambling out of the water. She shivered.

"Are you okay?"

Calla nodded. "Stupid river is deeper than it usually is."

"Now, Calla..." He began.

"It is! Try it yourself." She began to pout. "Grownups never believe me."

Perry frowned, and stuck his hand in the river. Strange, it was bigger than usual. And now that he thought about it, he had been walking on grass this entire time, when there was usually a dirt bank that he liked to walk along. That was much more than a simple rain swell, right?

"Is something wrong?" Calla asked.

"I'm not sure," Perry said. He wiped her face, and bundled up the poles under one arm. "You okay with me running ahead to the wall?"

Calla started sprinting ahead, ignoring the wet sneakers slapping on the grass. "Race ya!"

Perry wanted to laugh as he hustled after the girl. But it didn't seem to be something he wanted to joke about.

A quarter mile up the mountain side, they came to the glacier. Half buried in rock, it stretched halfway up the mountain cliffs. White ice jutted out of the rocks. Gravel ran up veins of ice. It was difficult to tell if the ice lay on the mountain, or there was simply rock burrowed into a frozen monument.

Perry skidded to a stop next to Calla, and stared up at the mountain. Calla leaned next to him, and huddled close.

"The glacier looks sick," She whispered.

It was the best description for the ice. Water that had once bubbled out of the bottom and the rock, now broke out in sweats all across the cliff face. There were ice chips sitting at the base of the mountain, and Perry could see where they had toppled from perches that had lasted centuries. If the rock could move, it most likely would have shivered.

Perry walked up to the glacier, and laid his hand on the side. He pressed his fingers in, and his hand disappeared into the white and blue. He pulled it out quickly, and almost yelped.

His hand was cold, but not unbearably so. It was like he stuck his feet into a river in December, not a tundra.

The glacier was melting, and *fast*.

"Calla, come with me," Perry said.

"But what about the-"

"Now!" He screamed. He threw the poles away, flung the girl over his back, and ran back towards Freedom.

Her clammy skin slapped on the back of his neck. His hair must have stood on end and stuck into her face. Perry couldn't believe what he was thinking. Glaciers melted, of course they did. But over years, decades even. Why did he think that it was disappearing now?

But he knew, he knew that it was coming, and soon. Not in a day, or a week. Perry thought it could be no more than hours. They might not even have that long.

Perry streaked into the town, and started screaming. "Everybody out! Out of bed, out of town!"

Cluny stuck his head out of his home. "Perry? What are you talking about?"

"The glacier is melting," Perry set Calla down.

"It's always," Cluny began, and Perry clutched the Frenchman's clothes.

"Not like this. The outside is nothing but slush, Cluny. Rocks are falling off the side."

"Perry, are you sure?"

"We need to get Freedom evacuated." Perry looked around. "Where is everyone?"

"Up at the mine," Cluny said. "Lucard is leading the expedition."

Perry started running. "Get Calla to safety!" He shouted.

"Where?" Cluny asked.

Anywhere. Anywhere but the valley. And the mine was going to be nothing more than a tomb filled to the brim with ice water.

A crash resounded, and Perry fell to the ground. Another crash, a dull thud that resounded against the trees. Water crested over the tree line, and fell back down behind the treetops.

Perry stood up. His breath caught in his throat, and he turned to Calla and Cluny. They looked up the river. Their eyes flashed with understanding.

"Calla!" Perry screamed.

The trees bent, and broke from their roots. A wall of water surged through. It was not white, not anymore. It was brown sludge that could outrace the wind. The town broke into kindling. The pieces joined the froth and moved onwards. It all rushed towards them.

Perry witnessed his two friends disappear beneath the water and muck. He caught a glimpse of fear from Calla before the muddy river caught him and tore the man off the ground. He spun away, off towards the rocks below.

Perry gulped down dirt and water, and spat it back out. His arms fought against the rocks and trees that tried to send him to the bottom. His legs kicked out, but he could already feel them weakening. *Not like this, please not like this.* He couldn't have survived that grave that was once Salt Lake City, only to drown in the truest home he ever had.

He can't. He won't end like this. He will not.

Perry blinked his eyes, and sunlight streamed forth in his eyes. He shut his eyes, and sat backwards. His back hit rock. Solid rock.

Perry almost fell off his perch, and looked around. He was above the glacier's first resting place. Up, up to the top of the mountain, settled on a wide ledge. How, how was he a mile away, upstream? Was it another terrible dream, was everything...

The glacier was gone. He leaned over the edge, and could see the melted ice floe run away from the mountain. What had once been the peaceful riverbed was a jumbled mess, trees floating away from their roots. Mud and dirt swirled in eddies down the mountain side towards the town.

No, it wasn't. The town was gone. Perry could see the river clearly now, with no trees in the way. Where the town once had been, there was thatch and timbers, already drifting away. In a few minutes there would be nothing that could be seen from the ground that could mark where Freedom once was.

Cluny was gone. Calla was gone. Perry looked on, and knew where the mine was. Underwater.

Lucard...

"Lucard!" Perry shouted it to the skies. Not again. Not another one. How could it be? Why did he have to survive? How did he, of all people, survive? It was impossible. It was pain.

"There is hope," a voice said.

Perry whirled around. There before him, was the impossible. Four figures stood there out of myth. A man sat on a rock, but with the head and claws of a tiger. Next to him, carrying an axe, was a dwarf, or a midget. A dark beard hung down his chest, and he glared ahead. Perry almost fainted when a Minotaur emerged, and stared down at him. Its chest was bare, but its bull head held a clasp on one horn.

And there, in front of him, was Calla's angel. She was just like the girl had described. She was winged, and kind, and calm. Perry sank to his knees and wept.

They were gone, all of them gone. And he was amongst the impossible.

"How did I live?" Perry asked.

The angel rushed up, close to him. "Magic, dear one." Her voice was soft, and reassuring. It spoke of hope.

"That's not real," Perry whispered. "You're not real."

"We are, and this is," She hung her head. "I am so sorry."

Perry looked up to her. "The world is damned."

The angel cradled his head, and tutted. "The world is saved, young man." She held him close. "With magic, with us, the world will grow. It will continue on. It will thrive."

Perry held her close, and tried to close his eyes. "Did I fly?"

"You did so much more," She said. "You were magic."

"How did it feel?" The dwarf asked.

"Like I could do anything," Perry said.

"You could," The Minotaur rumbled.

The angel nodded.

"I can do anything," Perry whispered.

"Yes," The angel said.

Perry dissolved in her hands. She stood up, and wiped herself off.

"Blech," Isda muttered. "Why do I have to be the one to touch those dirty things?"

"You were the one the little girl saw," Murken the dwarf said. "If you hadn't, we wouldn't have had to up the timetable."

"Besides," The Minotaur Kekrops said. "Mortals trust you more than all of us."

"Little flesh bags should just up and, ugh." Isda spread her wings and soared a few feet into the sky.

Murken looked towards the rakshasa Colavev. He hadn't spoken, and instead had looked out into the murk below.

"Did we get all of them?"

"Difficult to say," Colavev cracked his knuckles. "Humans are notoriously difficult to kill."

"Worthless things have a way of sprouting up," Isda began.

Kekrops slammed a hoof to the ground, and caused the other three to jump in surprise. He glared at the angel, and smoke flared from his nostrils.

"Do not speak of them as such," He growled.

"They're just humans," Isda muttered.

"They are sacrifice," Kekrops said. "We spill their blood for the sake of the earth. We snuff their life so that others may thrive. Their deaths are the noblest act of all."

Murken and Isda shared a glance. This was one of Kekrops' quirks. But he killed humans efficiently with no sense of remorse. Perhaps this was their first glance as to why.

"What now?" Isda asked Colavev.

The rakshasa stretched, and stood. He looked over the wreckage, and nodded.

"We wait until nightfall, and then go down and look for survivors."

"And then?" Kekrops asked.

Colavev shrugged.

"You know the rule. No survivors."

Adapted Armaments, The Last Bullet

Every shot counts. Coming down to the last of it, the last of an older power. If you waste it, if you cheapen it, there will be your legacy. As a fop rather than a fitting tribute.

Meechim never wanted to wax poetic out loud. As the team's sniper he felt it was in his job description to remain silent. Several of the new members had yet to hear him speak. In point of fact, Meechim only wanted to talk at meetings with Stryke team. He ate in the mess hall, slept in his bedroom (be it alone or not), and read reports in the library. With all of these goals, he tried to speak rarely, and with purpose.

Meechim almost never spoke during a job. He wanted to bring that number down. He could do it, too. If Nevie could keep still. Tilda needed to keep a lid on her, and maybe watch Retch and Lawg. The two were good, if careless.

The sniper snorted, and looked back at his weapons. That could describe Stryke team, and the entirety of Adapted Armaments. Mixed, careless, uptight, and ultimately effective. Tilda kept it that way. She knew how her teams worked in war.

Stryke Team was the best. It was an acknowledged fact for the rest of the teams. The others, like Felluge, Terran, Wyng, or Blaist, may claim they had skills that Stryke lacked. And in their environments they may have been superior. But Stryke could do it all, in any terrain, and was led by Tilda herself. There was no contest after that.

The team was then the best mercenary crew on the planet. Adapted Armaments was recognized as the premiere organization in this planet that had new for-hire houses springing up every few months. These new outfits could bring strength, or this new magic, or another new fad, but they didn't understand how war changed. Tilda did.

This was why Meechim was looking at both a sniper rifle and a modified bow. One was a bolt-action sniper, the fourth-generation of snipers post-Folly. Interchangeable barrels to accommodate both standard bullets, and musket rounds with incendiary spells. A simple spell and a ball of iron would shoot out of the barrel like it was chased by hellfire. For all that the sniper knew about the spell, it could be.

The bow was getting to be more his style. A compound bow that had been recovered from before the Folly, he spent most of his time training with this and the longbow that was being developed back at the house. Meechim was already proficient at five hundred yards. With a little training, he thought he could double that in six months, easy.

But today was the sniper. Tilda wanted it clean, and easy. No thinking about what could be the future. Today there was a noble and his entourage making the mistake of having rich enemies.

Time to get into position.

Adapted Armaments was founded five years ago by Tilda. She had fought in the Second Civil War of the Americas, after World War Three had descended into nothingness. She moved north as castles were coming back into fashion and people were discovering that magic was not just for the stage. Tilda Swain more than anyone seemed to know that magic was the future.

Which had made Meechim such an unusual pick, especially for the premiere outfit. As much as he was learning, he was a sniper. Hide away in a roost a few thousand yards off the beaten path. When Tilda found him squirrelled away in New Maya fighting the Aztec wars, he had never touched a spell, much less look at magic with anything higher than disdain.

But while magic was the future, guns were the present. Bullets were running out fast, being replaced by muskets that were being replaced by weapons that hadn't been in use since the Renaissance, but they were still effective. As long as there was a round in the clip, Meechim could place it within a millimeter of the target.

There was a round in the clip. Just one. If he needed more, there were musket balls and arrows in the modified quiver at his side. The rest of the one hundred, sixty four sniper-compatible rounds were sitting in a vault, under lock and key that neither he, nor Tilda, nor anyone of the team members had access to. That was one of the rules.

The most important rule to Tilda Swain was the one that everyone understood. "We do not judge." There was no sign above the house proclaiming the motto, no one muttered it as a rallying cry, or promise. The exact words were not even mentioned in the same sequence from telling to telling. But it was at the core of Adapted Armaments, and everyone recognized it. Signing on with Tilda Swain meant you checked your own morality at the door.

Even now, as Meechim set up his shot, he didn't know who this nobleman was. Right up the side of the mountain, looking down at the western wall. It was cooling down into sunset. No, it didn't matter. It didn't matter if he was a good man, or not even a man at all. Could be a woman, or a Fae, or anyone else that had started to pop up around the planet.

The only thing that mattered was that Tilda had two-thirds pay in advance. And that was enough to remove any thought of questions.

"I think this is a dumb job," Nevie muttered.

Damn it all, Nevie! The girl needed to understand silence. She was twenty years old, but this was a mission.

Tilda's presence settled on Meechim's mind, linking everyone together telepathically.

"Nevie, we have been over this in private." Tilda's voice in his head was still harsh. She was better with clients, but had little patience even in her mind for talking during a job. "The money and package were well within our price range."

"The noble..."

"Target." Meechim muttered.

Nevie's voice giggling in his head was worse than in person. "I got him, Lawg. You owe me."

"Damn it, Meech," Lawg said. "Keep communications down to a minimum."

"If we could all focus." Meechim looked down the scope, and located Tilda. The commander was tall, built like a bulldozer, and was planning something about as subtle. She leaned against a rock, just out of line of sight of the manse. An old building that had survived the war, a brick wall separated the grounds from the tree line. Thirty years ago there was a road, asphalt, leading to some billionaire's estate and back out to town. The town was gone, the billionaire as well. In its place was the target, who oversaw the surrounding lands.

For the next ten minutes or so.

"We're in position." Retch and Lawg were flat on their stomachs, just beyond the tree line. They stuck together, brothers in name if not in blood. There were rumors of many other things, ranging from the mysterious to the obscene. Meechim didn't know, didn't care. When they fought together, they protected the other man's back.

"Confirmed," Tilda looked around. "Nevie, where are you?"

"In the mansion."

Silence.

"Repeat?"

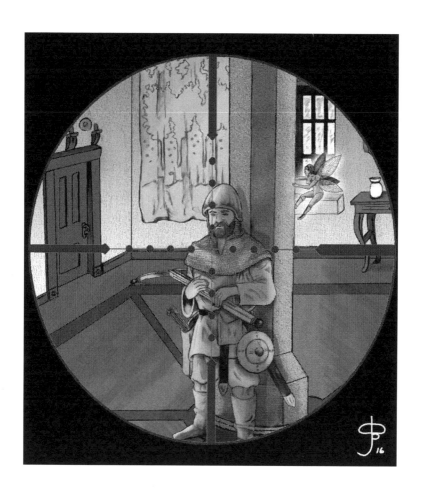

"I'm in the mansion, Tilda." Nevie's giggle had to be the worst thing Meechim heard. He picked up the sniper rifle, and was pointed at the assigned window before the commander could order him to do so.

"Damn it, Nevie!" Tilda turned away, her hand to her head. "You were on reconnaissance. Locate the target, and lay low."

"Pretty low right now. As low as I can go."

Meechim scanned through the windows and target areas. Couldn't find either the target or Nevie. She was understandable. If Nevie didn't want to be seen, she wouldn't be.

"Okay, okay, okay. Are you seen?"

"Tilda..."

"Nevie."

Nevie paused for a moment before answering. "I'm in position, commander. Under cover and not visible. Awaiting orders."

Good. There were times when Nevie went off task. Montreal, Alberta, the new Northwest Territories, damn that one hurt. But if Nevie could focus, they might have a shot of not dying.

"Number of guards?"

"I've seen twelve, mostly men-at-arms, swords, bows. Though I've seen one guy with a hammer, might give Lawg a run for his money."

Lawg snorted. He and Carlotta, his pride and joy, had decimated several competitions amongst the mercenary houses. He took great pride in his skill with the sledge. Meechim sent a quick prayer upwards to the unfortunate guard that he not come close to the brothers.

"Okay, let's do this with a velvet spike," Tilda muttered. She stretched, cricked her neck, and started up towards the main doors. Time to make a paycheck.

The unwritten rule was one that was hard to embody. Both in general, and for Tilda's case in particular. Each member of Stryke team, and most likely the rest of Adapted Armaments, had their opinions on the jobs taken. Even Tilda Swain must have considered turning down jobs based on the sheer humanity of their targets.

There was a question, even then, as Tilda knocked on the door. What was the crime that was committed? What so offended another being that this noble's existence had to end?

She came to the door. The countess Mont Real. An older woman, in her fifties. Tan skin, weathered by time, her gray hair hanging down in the latest fashionable braid. Malia Mont Real had amber eyes that regarded Tilda Swain with indifference.

Meechim always found that unusual. Even though Tilda was a good foot taller than the countess, Malia still found a way to look down on the commander.

"Tilda Swain," The countess murmured. "To what do I owe the pleasure?"

Tilde shrugged. "I think you know, countess."

Countess Mont Real nodded. She looked around, scanning the mountain and tree line. "I assume there are several men out there...four, if the reports are correct?"

"I'd rather not say, countess." Tilda said. "Their security, you know."

The countess shivered, clutching her chest. "Brisk evening. Would you like to come in?"

"We'll do it out here, if you please." Polite. Tilda always wanted to be polite, even on the jobs.

"Oh, shit. Tilda, we've got a problem."

Tilda didn't even twitch a muscle. She smiled, sat on the ground, and laughed. "You're good, countess." She laughed again, and turned around.

Meechim adjusted his sights. Retch and Lawg walked out of the tree line, hands above their heads. Three guardsmen walked behind them, while a fourth struggled with holding Carlotta in his grip.

"Have a shot," He muttered.

"Please, don't." Tilda held up her hands as well. "Countess, you know us, you've hired us. Please, can we be professional about this?"

"Professional?" The countess wound up and smacked her across the face. Tilda reeled back, and slammed her hand in the dirt.

"Professional? I hired you, you ungrateful little bitch." The countess almost frothed at the lips. "You were supposed to kill that peasant."

"And several dozen others you neglected to mention would be miffed about his death," Tilda said. She stood up, and grimaced. "You've got a strong backhand, countess."

"It was a peasant uprising. Some slag had misunderstood their place."

"And what about your place, Countess?" Tilda said. She glared ahead at the other woman. "What about when you, at the tender age of twenty, brought your money and your drug cartels north during the war, and conquered a people that just wanted to stay out of it?"

Meechim sighed. Tilda was breaking her rules again.

"I was under the impression it was not your policy to question a contract." The countess' arched eyebrow was enough for a guard to slug Tilda. The commander doubled over, but did not fall.

"We do not judge," Tilda began. They hit her again. Meechim wanted to squeeze the trigger. Do it now, get rid of everyone. He had his bow, and could go to it in seconds after he pulled the trigger.

"You do not judge."

"But this was not a question of judgment," Tilda said. "You hired us to kill one..." She looked at Retch. The wiry man shrugged. Meechim zoomed in, and noticed the stiletto that fell into the man's hand with the movement.

"I think his name is Calobar, a self-proclaimed prophet."

"Him." Tilda nodded. "Some styled prophet, trying in vain to build up a revolt against their 'tyrant bitch of a countess,' to quote."

If the countess squinted any more, she would close her eyes.

"I have no problem killing him, and the money was more than adequate. Here you go, by the way," Tilda tossed a money pouch on the ground. "Refunded in full."

"Squeamish?"

"I'm talking now." Tilda looked at Retch and Lawg, showing her back to the noblewoman. "I like my team. They do good work, and often go above and beyond their duties with aplomb. As such, I don't like putting them in unnecessary danger.

"Such as having to fight our way out of a horde of fanatics after we assassinate their leader. At last count, there were fifty-three peasants willing to die, and eager to kill any enemy of theirs."

"I thought you were the best."

Tilda's arms clenched. Dealing with this woman, having to talk with her, had to be more than a strain on her good nature. Meechim might have to kill Mont Real now, prevent anything messy.

"We *are*." Tilda breathed. "But you paid for one rebel leader, not putting down a fucking rebellion. You put us on expecting a grand fight that most likely would wipe out any opposition. And Adapted Armaments, for all its failings and quirks, is not in the business to do *freebies*, you self-centered bitch."

"Kill her," The countess turned away. "And make it slow."

"Oh, countess!" Tilda called out. "Does that mean our contract is ended?"

"Of course," She muttered.

Meechim pulled the trigger.

And the bullet jammed.

"Shit!" Meechim threw the gun down. He didn't bother with the mind spell, just grabbed the bow. "Retch, Lawg, move!"

The brothers shoved the guards to the ground. Lawg had Carlotta in his hands and swinging before the countess could move. Meechim had his bow in hand, sprinting down to the second perch. He needed to close the distance for range. They could hold off.

The sound of battle was in his ears as he ran through the trees. Tilda was unarmed, but adept in hand-to-hand combat. He could hear a few screams, broken bones…

"I'm here!" And Nevie bursting out of the window. The ten-inch pixie looked like a glowing ball of blue light as she cast sleep spells left and right.

Meechim reached the second perch, a bare outcropping of rock four hundred yards away. He drew an arrow from the quiver, nocked it and wounded a guard that was trying to creep up behind Lawg. Lawg looked down at the guardsman to see the hammer, and glared up at Meechim. That was supposed to be his kill.

"Stop!"

Countess Mont Real held Nevie in her grasp. The pixie bit at the noble's fingers, but the woman held firm.

"Drop your weapons or I crush this thing to putty," She breathed.

"Meechim," Tilda said. "If she so much as twitches, you have your second shot."

The sniper trained his bow on the countess. He looked at the distance, and swore under his breath. At this range, Malia would hear the twang of the bow, and have a breath to kill Nevie before the arrow found her target.

There needed to be a better way.

"You don't do vengeance missions, Swain," Malia Mont Real snarled. "What the hell are you doing, killing my guards and trying to assassinate me?"

"Somebody ponied up the money."

"Who?"

"That little prophet." Tilda shrugged. "Turns out prophets are better-off than their cause."

"Knew it," Malia said.

Tilda looked at the remaining guards. "There's about to be a regime change, regardless of whether or not you kill us. We're here, we're ready to die, and the countess is going with us. You can kill us, but you'd just be signing your own death sentences with the new order."

"They even so much as breathe wrong, kill them!" Malia screamed.

Meechim shot again. Arrows don't jam until they reach their target.

The guards stared blankly at the countess. Swords were drawn, gripped loosely, awkwardly. Retch pushed one out of a swordsman's grip. He didn't notice. He stared at his lady, laid out in front of her door, and arrow between her eyes.

Nevie grunted, and struggled, punching at the fingers holding her. "A little help here!" She shouted. "Before she tightens up!"

Lawg pried the death grip loose, letting the pixie out. Nevie flit around, looking at each of the team members in turn.

"Meechim is psycho," she muttered. "Good, but psycho."

"I can hear you, Nevie," The sniper said. He picked his way back to his stash. Up the mountain.

Lawg hefted Carlotta, and looked around the guards. "Are we going to have a problem?"

No response. Nevie shook a finger in their faces, and nodded. "Well, there! No messing with us. I know pixie judo. It's even better."

Tilda sighed. "Nevie, there is no such thing as pixie judo."

"I made it up!" Nevie said. "It's even better."

"Why were you even in on this mission?" Retch said. The rest of Stryke team walked up the mountainside to rendezvous with Meechim. "You basically snuck into a mansion and then screamed."

"I am sneaky, and know things." Nevie said. "Things that no one else can find out."

"Oh, yeah?"

"Yeah," Nevie stuck her tongue out at him. "I know why Lawg calls his hammer Carlotta."

"And you're keeping quiet about that," Lawg said. "Before I play whack-a-pixie."

Nevie giggled. She flew ahead, and lit on Meechim's shoulder as he looked over the rifle. "So what happened?"

"Hmmm?"

"You totally almost killed us back there."

"Nevie," Tilda scolded. "Not the time."

"Accurate," Meechim pulled the bullet out of the gun, and looked at it. Sure enough, the firing pin worked, everything went like it had ten thousand times before.

"Dud?" Tilda asked.

"Becoming more common," Meechim said. There had been stories of whole magazines misfiring now. Whether that was because they were being scammed by the black market, or magic, was anybody's guess. But it was happening.

He stared at the bullet. A perfect mark, dead-center of the casing. Some of his finest work. Maybe his last.

He stuck the round in his pocket. He promised himself to fashion it into a necklace. From now on he was sticking with his bow. It was more dependable than a gun.

He'd miss it. The feel, the ease, the satisfying pop. But it was time to forget the past. Guns were just outdated.

<u>Magical Poetry</u>

<u>3 Spells gone Awry</u>

1.

Magic means the world,
Inspired to spin anew
And then gives me hats…

2.

They shall all burn. In fire, *igni, Hie.*
This spell I weave, yes, listen to my cry.
For this, this world is filth best turned to ash.
Let this glass globe quiver, and quake, and crash.

Let fall! The mighty are the kindling, Hale
And dry. I call upon the wrath of tale.
Let magic guide this folly. Yes, the spells
Will hold the world, for its descent to hells.

I will?
Let spill?
Till I've had my fill.

Magic?
   That's me.
      But, what? What life is this before
My eyes? Neither substance, figure nor form.
Yet, lest the mind and soul deceive, I feel
A presence, mind that is above the real.
      You're so sweet.

Spell! Mistress of power and might, let loose
Your strength upon a world who
        Nah.
…*what?*
Orange is not my favorite color.
Neither is ashen gray.
So I'm not destroying the world.
Nope, not today.

I command

You command? You dare command magic?
Who art thou, to command the force that laughs
At such petty constructs as lifes and deaths?
This petty wizard before me is nothing more than

An insignificant speck who should have ran
The moment he heard my
VOICE.

To keep this rhyme scheme, a choice.

Do you command magic, little man?
Magic heard no answer, he's still running as fast as he can.

3.

It has been decided,
All is for naught.

Puppies!
Puppies are now green,
And fly on every other Sunday.

They see all,
Know everything
And serve the Lord of Uncomfortable Darkness.

Puppies are now cats.
Until they get over it.

- Sincerely, the universe according to Blue.

A New Path

The books were hidden well. I could not
Imagine the power within.
My enemies already
Surrender. Life's a path
Of moves, counter-moves
Until one day
You grasp the
Will to
Change.

Spell Song

Catch the moment of a spell's first breath.
See it, hold it, magic in hand,
In tongue, enraptured in soul.
Can we measure the birth
Of such a wonder?
Or do we just
Lie and say
"Become
Now"?

4.

wind,
water,
earth and fire.
Dancing for us
In discontentment
Until we break the bonds
Of elements. Do they live
As we perceive? Or does this world
Mean less and more to the frail ways of
Earth?

Lich's Lament

I am the lich
The dead wizard.
An enemy to all that
"love life."

My adoration for life
Is absolute.
I cannot abide
Without the sweet
Scent of rebirth.

People hate my choice
The sick scrag of
Skeletal visage
That is me.

One day I will
Unlock the secret.
Breathe new life
Into tattered bone
And return to light

Or not. Remain
In this tomb, dank
And still.
Be the blight you think.

I am cold.
And alone, and afraid.
Will somebody
Please. Know me?

Sonnets

1.
I witnessed life explode, enflamed and born
A phoenix, ashen-faced and smiling.
Go, look upon this glowing child of morn
Her face is kind, sincere and beguiling.

The beauty is beyond knowledge, of tears
That fall from weary worldly creatures' eyes.
In prayer, in thanks and memory of fears
Now gone, lost, faded in this magic's rise.

A summer day, become still more wondrous
The gold has blended violet and teal
And crimson peals that ring yes, more thunderous
Tis sight, and sound, all sense that is more real.

But hark, with all the wonders we have seen.
Atomic bombs have wakened magic's dream.

2.
Let us consider wealth, wealth of nature
It's fickle, rise and fall, till its rebirth
Gives way to new, a life that has mature
Resolve, until it knows the truth of worth.

We look upon a painted cloud, and think
"It must be less real than imagined sky,"
How to respond? With words, a pen to ink
A dream that has slowly floated on by?

Reality. A hard word to withstand.
Illusion, fantasy comes by so fast.
Will we, humans, look at the breadth of lands
As self, a being that intends to last?

The world does not give me a hint of truth.
Perhaps it shall, when I have left my youth.

Lost Heroines

We all remember when the bombs fell. When the world was consumed in blood and ash. A century of violence, every man destroying his sister and brother for the last little resource left to them. Wars were fought until we lost track of who was fighting, and for what.

The true tragedy was when we lost the books.

I picked my way through the woods. The sun had just crested over the oaks, and if I wanted to get the work done before they left, I needed to hurry.

The staff was right where I left it, tucked away right by the brook. The branch had bumped into me when I ran here a few months ago. Tears had been in my eyes, and I couldn't breathe except to stifle a sob. Nothing had been fair. I'd stood in the brook, determined to let it just carry me away to the sea, or the Wastes. Anywhere would have been better than home.

Instead, a branch had snapped over the brook, and hit me in the shoulder. I lashed out, looking for an unseen enemy, but there was only a stick. No, more than that. It floated in the water. It shimmered, catching the light that broke through the leaves.

That was three months ago. The branch was now a staff, almost. I just needed to finish the final rune work. I sat on the bank, and dipped my toes into the water. Cool, as always, with just a hint of glow. My new home.

Books were the first thing to go during the war. Paper burned, and it wasn't until the fighting stopped that we finally realized what we sacrificed to kill each other. The worst thing was, so many books had been burned that we didn't even know what was lost.

My family is one of the few in town that has a library, of sorts. Shakespeare survived, and the Bible could be found in almost every home. But my family was different. My great-great-grandfather had collected comic books.

Those were the bedtime stories for generations. Great heroes that flashed through the sky. They stopped wars, destroyed the bombs, made sure the world was safe.

It was fiction, and every McKay knew this at the start. But it gave us a hope that someday, the heroes would come. And even if they didn't, we always had a story that was all ours.

There. I held the staff up, and smiled. The rune work was basic, but it would do. I had had to grab every tome and lesson from even the maddest wanderer that stumbled into town. Some of the symbols did nothing. Some I had to scrap because they were too dangerous. The others were on my staff.

I looked at my reflection in the water. My hair was braided, something mother always called a bright flame in the trees. My face was smooth, even when I frowned. Too kind, and I had to wear bulky clothes. I didn't want my curves to distract from what I was doing.

But the staff never wavered. That was good, and I had time. I could get back.

I knew the heroes would never come. I had known for years. There was radiation enough, but no one rose out of the ashes to save the planet. No heroes falling from a dying star, or out of the depths of the shadows and sea. That was yesterday's hero.

I spoke a word, and the staff glowed. I grinned, and rubbed the surface.

My name is Emelia McKay, and I have something better than superheroes. I have magic.

The sun was shining, and there wasn't a single cloud in the skies. I knew it was going to lead to trouble. Good.

It isn't as simple as I thought it to be. I live in a quiet little town, by a little brook, with little people leading little lives. In fact, the name is Littlebrook. As imaginative as could be hoped for in a town populated almost entirely by farmers and woodsmen. But the tavern was always homey, the store was well-stocked, and the people were kind to a fault.

I leaned against my staff, testing its weight. There was a slight bend, but it wasn't supposed to be stone. And it didn't seem anyone noticed when I walked through town.

"Hey Emelia!"

"Young lady, are you supposed to be working on the dairy?"

"Light of my life..." No. Not that one. No one had anything of value to say. But they were running towards their duties, either towards the farmlands, or to the store to drop off goods.

Littlebrook is human, for the most part. Magic sent a few others our way. But magic's been around enough that an elf or gnome wandering through doesn't faze us. It's when they try to stay that eyebrows are raised. But once someone puts down roots, they become part of the community. And hellfire will be raised if anyone tries to step in from the outside to bring harm.

Except for the Snake River Boys.

They were in town, that much was easy to know. For one, they could be heard in the tavern. I stepped lightly onto the main street, a little dirt gash through the stone and wooden buildings. Stopping for a rest by the barber shop. Catch my breath, and look around for the Boys.

I spotted their mounts. The Boys always looked for something a little more exotic. There were horses, to be sure, but the new members would trade them in for the special ones. Mares that had nubs at the shoulder blades, or a tail that fell to the ground. Even a stub of a horn was found on two of the steeds.

The women in the Boys were, if anything, more exotic. Maybe they needed to stand out. But if the steed looked like anything except a horse, chances were it was a woman. Not that it mattered to Scales if his Boys weren't all men. The only requirement was ruthlessness in battle.

Magic was hitting everything, and everyone. Myths that had once just remained on the page, were stepping out into life. In another few decades, would those nubs become wings? The scaled one, would he become more lizard than horse?

I stiffened, and looked at the wolves. They stood taller than me at just the shoulder, a pair of males that challenged everything with their mere presence. Dire wolves were the first to break out of the wild, and taming them was considered both a feat and insanity.

The Dire Brothers were here. Which meant Scales was in town.

My grip tightened around my staff.

The armory was having a sale when I walked past. Whenever the Snake River Boys were in there was a sale throughout Littlebrook. They were having a great time, and I hated it.

The Boys are always around twenty strong. Professional protectors of ours and a half-dozen other towns around the Snake River and its waterways. To their credit is a resume of fighting anyone who tried to come close to their territory. Elves, fairies, even the dwarves never once laid a hand on our hills. Anyone who tried to take over what we spent generations trying to build was sent packing with their tail between their legs. Everything we had was ours, and the Boys made sure of that.

We just had to help them along every once in a while.

Littlebrook really is just one street. It's not paved, there are just some cobblestone sidewalks for convenience, or to put one of the kids to work who was looking like trouble. A few buildings, less than a dozen on each side. Some were stone, others brick, but most were wood with porches jutting out towards the dirt.

I sat on the porch for the barber shop. The Boys were milling about, laughing as they loaded up the horses. It was a good day, well-lit and in a good town. They walked with Fredric, the store owner. They were always polite, and Fredric laughed whenever they ran into town.

It was easier for superheroes to pick out the villains in a crowd. I couldn't. The entire horde wasn't just some organization of bastards. In fact, the Boys for the most part were polite. No, they were more than polite, they were friendly, almost loving. Rensen and Carl had homes here. They sent money back for their wives and children. One of the girls...Shirley, I think, spent her days off fishing with the kids.

And if I had my way, they'd never come by here again. I asked myself again, was I about to do the right thing? If everyone was just like the Dires and Scales, would I be thinking this way? Or would I be too scared to move?

There was a smell of dog. The Dires walked out of the tavern.

Walked out. The Dires never walked when they could prowl. Sleek, dressed in black leathers and cotton, they let their strides slide with their gaze. There was a smirk on Davey's face, while Tranc scowled. Both had been drinking, but Davey must have been winning poker at his brother's expense.

The brothers were best described as wolf-like. Even rumored to have one as an ancestor. With this much magic, it was difficult to tell if that were just a story, or true. They sure acted the part, dark hair that hung down past their necks. And when they tore into a meal, it made one want to check their teeth. Just not too closely.

Unlike any of the other Boys, the Dire brothers never carried weapons. Between them and their dogs, they didn't need them.

If the Dires were in the saloon, Scales must be just behind them. And there he was, bursting out of the bar. Dragging my dad with him by the scruff of his shirt.

No. no, he was supposed to let it go. Mom said she was going to talk him down.

She rushed out right after Scales. Her apron flew out behind her. Her hair was frazzled, and tears streamed down her face. No, mom. Don't make a scene. Scales wants to make a speech, a spectacle. Don't let him.

Scales loved a speech, loved being imposing. He kept the Dires next to him, just for the contrast. Where they were sleek and furry, the leader of the Snake River Boys was bulked and bald. Not a hair on an inch of his physique. Extremely muscled, it bulged out of his vest. Both arms were bare, to better show off the hairless body he took such pride in.

A tattoo of a dragon ran down the length of his right arm. Scales claimed it was an ancestor. I didn't know what to think of it. Just let my dad go.

He looked pathetic next to Scales. The leader's hand could wrap all the way around his neck. His face was red, could he breathe? His arms lashed out, hitting those muscles. Scales almost seemed to enjoy it.

"Brent, Brent, Brent," Scales muttered. He looked around, and everyone silenced. Scales was about to make a speech.

"Why can't you just play along? We like you, hell, I like you. You're a good bartender. Always let my boys in, never gave a fuss. Why are you talking about something so hurtful as debts now?"

Dad gurgled. Mom sobbed. Davey Dire moved a step closer to mom.

"No, Davey," Scales said. "Let Mary watch. She should have stopped her husband from being so... just so disappointing."

He relaxed his grip, and dad gulped down air. My dad collapsed to the ground, and rolled onto his back, gasping.

I looked around, seeing if anyone was going to do anything. The Boys traded glances, and then gazed at all of my neighbors. Almost daring one of them to make a move. No one did.

Scales squatted down, and looked at dad. "Now, we do you a good turn, more than a good turn, Brent." He waved his hand down past the road. "There are goblin raiders, elves, dwarves...not to mention whatever crawls out of those Wastes."

Tranc snorted, and showed his teeth.

"We're out there, out in the wilderness day after day, just to make sure you have a good life. All I ask in return is a little meal, a drink here and there, and to make sure we can do our jobs."

He helped dad up, dusted him off. "Now, can we just go back to doing that?"

Dad looked him in the eye. "Did Davey touch that girl?"

Scales sighed. His fist lashed out, and crushed dad's face in.

Mom screamed, and ran towards her husband. Davey made a grab for her, but Scales held a hand up. The Dires let mom crowd around dad. She cradled his head to her chest, blood and flesh peeling off into her clothes. She screamed again.

"Anybody else have something to say?" Scales shouted.

I stood up. I guess that was my cue.

I placed a hand in my shirt, and pulled out a green strip of cloth. I tied it over my face, two slits letting me see without difficulty. I gripped the staff, and steeled myself.

"Sc-Scales!" Dammit.

His head whipped towards me, and that glare was what got to me. I just watched my dad die. And this bastard, this piece of dragon slime was the one who killed him. He wasn't going to leave.

I took a step forward. I shook all over, hoping it wasn't showing. Too important not to keep going.

Scales sneered at the little girl walking towards him. "Who are you supposed to be?"

I stopped on the opposite side of the street. "Scales, you've hurt the last person in Littlebrook."

He shrugged. "Didn't hurt him. His brains were gone before it really started to hurt."

I showed teeth, and tried not to growl. Dad was going to die, he always was going to. Once he decided to talk about Lacy in public, he was gone. Nothing was going to change that, and nothing did.

Scales stood up, and smiled. "Is that you, Emelia? Little Melly?"

Dammit twice. Secret identities are a lot harder when everyone knows your face. And I had had a Green Avenger speech all prepared. But Scales had to go and ruin that.

He laughed when I removed the mask. "It is! Oh, Melly, I'm sorry you had to see that." He motioned to my mother. "Mary, why don't you go with your daughter, go on home."

Mary stared at me. Her eyes were dead, uncomprehending. Whatever reason she had had, was in her arms with dad. I don't think she could have moved if a stampede was rolling straight towards her.

Scales motioned to the staff. "That's a pretty thing for a pretty girl. You carve that yourself?"

I pointed it straight at him. "Scales, you and your wolf friends, pack up and leave. Never come back to Littlebrook. I won't ask you twice."

The shaking was getting even harder to control. I needed to focus, not on Scales and his size. On the rune work, on the oak in my hand. If he moved, I knew it had to be quick.

Sure enough, Scales smiled. He moved towards me. "Let's have a talk."

Superheroes only had one stupid habit. They let the villains off with warnings. It was mercy, right for such a civilized world. They lived in a land of laws, order. Higher values and ideals to be aspired to. Here good isn't reached for, but clawed after. And magic's given me talons.

I screamed my curse, and lashed out with the staff. All the rage burned out of me, straight down the staff and blazed out in an emerald fire at Scales.

It engulfed the bastard. For all his vaunted dragon blood, he cried out as the flames burned his flesh. The sound gave me fuel, gave me strength. I shouted again, and the fire redoubled its efforts.

The smell of burning cotton filled the air. Around me I could feel both the Boys and the townsfolk watch in agony. They couldn't turn away, couldn't bear to not see this.

Before I knew it I had to breathe again. I gasped, the spell ending in an instant. The staff almost shook out of my hand. I gripped it tighter, and let my arm jolt back and forth. I spasmed in front of the town.

"Henh."

My gaze snapped up. There Scales stood. Blackened, the clothes flaked away to nothing as they clung to his skin. He wavered, and collapsed on his back. He grunted, and sat up.

"I'm the dragon," He muttered.

I hit him again. And again, and again. Fire poured out of me, forces of wind, it streamed out of my body towards that thing that dared step on my street. He killed my dad, I didn't want him to even exist anymore!

In the end, when I couldn't move anymore, there was nothing left that could be called Scales. A smear, that's what remained. A smear of blood and charcoal that stretched from a scorch of embers that still flickered in the dying sun. When I got my strength back, I was going to get a bucket of water and wash that away, too.

My body was broken inside. It howled in pain. I needed to sit, to lay down on the dirt and just die for a while. I had beaten him, beaten the dragon.

But the minions were still there.

I leaned on the staff, and pointed my free hand at the rest of the Boys.

"Now." I breathed. "Get out."

The Dires howled. A low, keening sound that grew in volume till it broke against my eardrums. Their hands lengthened, fingers becoming claws. Behind them a few of the Boys hefted swords, crossbows, and wands. They started towards me.

I hoped they'd see what happened to Scales, and just leave. Mostly. The Dires had too much to answer for. I put my hand to my mouth, and whistled.

There was one thing about heroes that they did understand.

The roofs rattled, and everyone's eyes looked upwards. They were behind me, but I knew they were there.

My team was assembled. And just spoiling for a fight.

Echo struck first. She had found a way to bend and mask all traces of herself. Sound, light, she could even disguise her own scent...though that was less about magic and more about rolling in sawdust and rosewood in preparation. Before the Dires knew what had happened she had stuck a silver blade in Davey's ribs. He howled, and tore her throat out in one gash.

Tranc was at his brother's side in a moment. It was far too late, for either him or Echo. She laid right next to the wolf, their blood pooling together in the dirt. No one besides Tranc wept for Davey. He had taken so much from Echo, taken as his due for the protection.

She had told me this was how she wanted to go. There was nothing for her but pain. She even felt a kick in her stomach, a parting gift that she had never wanted. Echo finally repaid Davey, and took his life first.

"Wahoo!"

I smiled. The fire bug twins flamed onto the scene, setting down on the roofs in a blaze of glory in bravado. Fila was dressed in orange, her brother Nare was too, and if Fila hadn't recently hit puberty I honestly couldn't tell them apart. Their smiles, glaring red hair, and talent for pyromancy were just too identical. Especially since they used the same hand motion to set Tranc on fire. He yelped, and started to run.

"Get back here!" Nare shouted after the Dire brother. He snapped his finger, and a whip of fire trailed down from his fingers. "We were just getting warmed up!"

Fila rolled her eyes. She never was one for puns.

The Snake River Boys were scum, for the most part. I was sure of this. But they knew how to fight. The twins had to duck away as arrows and knives were thrown up. And even a few realized I was still there, exhausted after killing their boss. Oh, no.

I stumbled away, and tripped over my feet. I was spent. I doubted I could move up to the barber's if I wanted to.

One of the Boys walked over, sword in hand. Perrin, was that his name? Damn it, one who was good with a blade. I couldn't even lift the staff.

I coughed. "Maybe make this sporting, give me a few minutes to compose?"

Perrin shrugged. "Sure. Same as you gave Scales."

Double damn it. "Shouldn't you help your friends?"

"They'll handle those- what the hell is that?!" he screamed, and backpedaled as something flew down.

The creature stood four feet tall. Coated in a light brown fur, she appeared shorter as she squatted in front of me. She stared at Perrin, and screeched. He backed away, and ran.

She turned to look at me. A face that would have been that of a young girl's, it was marred by a bat snout and black eyes. Her ears stuck out from under her close-cropped hair.

"He didn't like me, Mel," She said.

"I know, Lana," I said. I stood up, and leaned against the staff. "He's just a dummy."

It wasn't Lana's fault she looked that way. Her parents had ventured too close to the Waste, that scar of radiation that was once called New York. Lana had been born different, and was always going to be such. No matter that she could fly, and was the sweetest twelve-year-old anyone could ask for.

A purple blade tapped my staff. Good, Sela was here.

"Sela," I said. I looked at the blade. "Does that mean sir Violet is ready to play?"

A woman ran her hands over the blade. She was twenty-three, pale, lithe with the kind of silver hair that seemed too good to be real. Sela was dressed in her duelist clothes, complete with the scabbard at her side for sir Violet.

"Sir Violet has been told that this is how life must go," Sela murmured. She darted forward, and caught a sword in a parry. The two weapons were inches from Lana's back.

"He is much more satisfied with running through such knaves that dare attack a lady of good repute," Sela spun and stabbed Violet through the neck of one of the Boys.

"He wonders about your hearing, and apologizes for any crude language," Sela said. "But I would like to just kill some people. May I do that, Emelia?"

I nodded, and leaned against the staff. "Stick close to me, Lana," I commanded. The girl huddled next to me. "But don't look away. Don't shut away from reality. Accept it, and then move on to something better."

I didn't want Lana in the fight. She had been through her own share of scraps. If she ever ventured too far from Littlebrook, around strangers, they thought she was a bad omen. A sign of danger. I now knew the best way to mend a broken wing.

Broken. Everything seemed broken. My neighbors looked on in horror as Sela and the twins tore through the Snake River Boys.

The twins were dangerous, but Sela was skilled. Anyone who didn't want to get cooked soon realized that Sela had won the duelist's cup downriver for six straight seasons. And with sir Violet's permission, she was allowed to vent her strange anger against unknown enemies. She dismembered her opponents with a question on her face. I don't know if she truly understood what life was, or what happened to someone who lost an arm.

I cleared my throat, and tried to speak. "Enough," I croaked. I was even more tired than I thought, if I couldn't even shout.

Tranc was dead, the Dires and Scales were gone. There wasn't a reason to fight.

"Stop…" Weariness was settling in. Darkness clouding the vision, no! I was not going to pass out at this point.

"Lana," I leaned against the staff, and grimaced. "Wake everyone up, please."

Lana screeched. The sound was nails against the stones, right in my head. I fell, and clutched my head. Just keep conscious, that's all I needed to do.

I looked up, and everyone else was also on the ground. The twins held onto each other, while the Snake River Boys just rolled on the street, groaning. The windows wavered, threatening to shatter.

Lana stopped, and nodded. "Got them, Mel."

"That's true." I stood up. Nope, not happening. Lana was at my side, holding me up. "Now."

One of the boys leaped up, and sliced a sword across Fila's neck. She clutched at the neck, and looked at Nare. She didn't understand. She was supposed to survive, be happy. They were heroes.

Her blood matched her hair.

Fila wasn't supposed to die. Echo was, she wanted to die. Maybe me, too. I brought them together, and certainly deserved it for killing a man in cold blood. But Fila, no, she was life. She joined us because being a hero was fun. She would get a chance to help people, with her brother.

Nare held her head close. His mouth moved, whispering in his sister's ear. The man with the sword raised his hand again. Nare snapped his fingers. A blast of heat, and his sister's killer was ash.

Nare glared ahead, radiating heat. He held his sister close, and closed his eyes. No, Nare. Don't, please don't do that, it's too much.

He exploded. A wave of flame consumed a dozen of the Boys before lighting the porches on fire. It was gone in an instant, just enough to start the fires going. The armory was sparking, but the tavern was more wood than stone.

"Get up!" I screamed. "The street will go up. Get the buckets!"

Sela ran off, picking up a bucket along the way. Lana raced after her. The Boys looked at me in confusion, and I had to turn and hobble after the girls. They lapped me twice, laden down with a full pail of water splashed against the fire.

I made it to the river, and Sela tapped me on the shoulder. I collapsed against the added weight, and fell into the river. Water, water all around me. Soaking in, oh good.

I could think. Maybe if I lay down here, my problems would go away.

A hand snaked in, and gripped me by the wrist. No, just let me be nothing for a while. I needed to be numb, before I went back up to the town. I wanted to be away, far away before the reality sank in. about how many people I sentenced to death.

But the hand was firm, and I didn't particularly want to drown. Sela pulled me up out of the water. With a plop, she set me on the bank, and started to wring out my clothes while I was still in them.

A rush of wind, and Lana was by our side. She sat next to the two of us.

"We won," she said. Sela and I exchanged a glance. We survived, which I don't think was on either of our minds. I had walked into that fight sure that Scales was going to kill me, and I would just get enough of him to let the rest finish the job. Sela, Echo and I would take the bastards with us. The twins and Lana would not even be needed. It was a good plan, just completely stupid.

"How many?" I asked.

"There are maybe a half-dozen of the Boys left," Sela said. Her voice was soft, mechanical. "Somehow we saved the good ones."

"They were the ones with enough sense to not get involved." I raised a hand, and the girls helped me to my feet.

"Ready to survey the damage?" Sela asked. When I nodded, she started to walk with me in tow. I turned, and Lana was huffing behind us, gripping the staff.

Another thing superhero stories never truly got right was how much carnage there was in a battle. There would be rubble, and some broken bones, but too often buildings were either completely destroyed or not a scratch. First thing I saw was the burns. A scorch marked where the firebug twins laid. A pair of blackened skeletons, curled around each other. I wondered if Nare's last thought was wondering if he was really fireproof.

The blood was next. It wasn't just in the streets, it splashed against the posts of the buildings, the walls, the porches. Soaked into the street. Sela had been quick and vicious. Was it possible to trace her steps through the fight, following one patch of blood to another?

The townsfolk couldn't speak. Our neighbors started shouting, hands raised in protest. The remaining Boys reached for weapons. No, I didn't want to fight. Not again.

I raised my hands. "Peace, please."

"Peace?" one of the Boys stood up, a woman in her thirties. Her blonde hair was matted with dirt and ash. "You and your friends just slaughtered us. You want peace now?"

"Always," I said. "Just not with Scales and the Dires."

"You killed my friends!" She screamed. "I'm going to gut..."

Sela drew sir Violet, and raised the sword up. "If I wanted, six more bodies would be on the ground," She murmured. "If Emelia wanted, I wouldn't even get close enough to wet sir Violet."

They stared at her in contempt.

"We were just trying to help," Lana said. She huddled behind the two of us, and passed the staff to me. I gripped it, held on for strength.

"What the hell did we ever do to you?" one of the Boys, a man this time, asked.

I shrugged. "Nothing to me. Not until Scales decided to kill my dad to make a point. Remember that?"

I pointed to my mother. She hadn't moved from in front of our tavern. Her dress was scorched, blackened, and there must have been some sparks that caught in her hair. It smoked, but if it irritated her, she ignored it. She just held onto her husband.

"How about when Echo was taken 'in payment,'" I asked. "Or any of you took a free meal as your due?"

I looked at mom. She was dead inside, I knew that. She was going to waste away, without dad. But that had nothing to do with what I did. Just what I had to do.

"We're leaving," I said. "Me, Sela...Lana."

"We're just going to let you go?" one of my former neighbors called out.

"You want us to stay?"

Silence. I thought so.

I probably should've said goodbye. But would mom have heard me? Was there anyone else I really needed to say farewell to? The only ones I cared about were right next to me.

We went to where Lana had packs left outside of Littlebrook. She knew she was going to leave, but there were six bags. We had to leave some behind, the boy clothes, anything Echo and Fila liked. I searched through my bag, and stopped.

"Lana, you grabbed the comic books?"

She smiled, and hugged me. "Helps us find the way."

I ruffled her hair. Yeah, they'll help along the way.

Sela looked over one of the books, and picked it up. "You mind if I read this one?"

"Go ahead," I smiled. "We're in this together."

Sela rifled through it, and frowned.

"What's a slayer?"

Lost Heroines, Namesake

"I want to be Batgirl!"

"No!" I was adamant on this point. I had been adamant about it when Lana had found the book squirrelled against one side of the pack. Still adamant for the next few weeks, right up till yesterday when we reached Leftarch. Lana was not going to be named Batgirl.

Lana pouted, and almost stuck her tongue out. "Not fair. I even look like it."

To be fair, she did. The young girl had light brown fur poking out of her red tunic – fur I knew covered every inch of her. So even in the noonday sun, she wore a red cloak with the hood up, covering the bat like ears, black eyes and upturned snout. If there was anyone going to be called Batgirl, it was her.

But no, that was wrong. "You need your own name, Lana," I explained. "Something that captures all of you, not just what you look like."

Sela leaned against the tavern table. "Besides, it is in the books. You can't use a name that's in the books."

"That's not…"

"Yes it is!" Lana almost raised her voice, and stopped. We weren't in our room in town. We were a floor below, in the taproom, trying to get some much needed water and stretching done. But even then, we didn't want to draw too much attention to ourselves.

To Lana. We couldn't draw any to her.

She huffed, and sat in her chair. "You pay too much attention to the books," She muttered.

I shrugged. It was a criticism, but I didn't care. The books had given us clarity, and they would stay. I needed them to help guide our path.

Sela's hand trailed to the blade at her hilt. Sir Violet was probably whispering something in her ear. I could scream and she would just nod and turn away.

"What do the books say now?" Sela asked. "We have reached a metropolis. Do we save it?"

A metropolis. Leftarch was well over five thousand inhabitants strong. There was a city wall, three four-story buildings, and even a few banks. All surrounding a great arch that stretched far beyond the clouds, hence the name.

Names. Lana was right, we needed names. I was thinking the Green Witch for myself. But Sela would only grunt at any suggestions of mine. And Lana could not get away from Batgirl…

"The Green Witch is not a good name," Sela said.

"How did you...it's a fine name!" I hissed. "Green is my color."

"I want to be Stryke," Sela said. I could hear the 'y' in it, and hated it. "Or Sir Violet suggested the Wielder."

"No, no." I said.

"Batgirl is sounding better, now, isn't it?" Lana asked.

"No it isn't!" I said. "We can't just..."

The door banged open. A man stumbled forward, clutching his shoulder. It sparked lightning, striking the frame as he tumbled across the floor to the bar. He rolled onto his back, and coughed once.

"We've got elves."

Elves? Sela tried to adjust herself, and sat down in a chair slowly. All three of us tried to both turn away and listen close as the man was helped to his feet.

"Elves?" the bartender handed the man a drink. The injured one leaned against the bar, and took a drink. "They know better than move this far into the plains."

"Not these," The man said. "Psychotics. Mad savages who don't understand what territory means."

"That sounds..." Sela kicked me under the table. My hands went up and I almost spilled my drink everywhere. Lana gave a little yip. We all shushed each other.

"Pointy-eared bastards," The man muttered. "Was guarding a pilgrim party down the river, and they filled us full of arrows before anyone started screaming."

"Ain't right," Someone muttered. "Mindless beasts, killing decent folks."

I looked into my glass. Everyone knew that there were some elves that went wild, especially outside of what was Europe. They were skilled, dangerous, and hated anything that wasn't elven.

Maybe we could help. Yes! The perfect opportunity to get some real good done. A chance to make a difference.

"Are we helping them?" Lana asked.

"We sure are." I said.

Lana nodded, and got up. I grabbed her arm, eyes wide.

"What are you doing?"

"Talking with him?" Lana asked.

"Not yet!" this is something that required reverence. The best thing to do was slink away. Wait for the cover of darkness. What we really needed was to find a fabric shop and at least get masks. Domino-style was good, better was the other kind that covered the bottom half.

"Does getting rid of them pay?"

We turned to see a crossbowman lean against the bar. His weapon strapped to his hip, he looked the injured man over.

"Not much," The first man muttered. "But this is about women and children."

The newcomer nodded, and looked back to his table. Arrayed were five or six men. All were seedy-looking, and had never understood the meaning of the word bath. They looked way too cool not to take the job.

"We're probably suckers, but let's get you another drink."

A cheer went through the bar. The two men walked back, and Sela glared in my direction.

"That was supposed to be us." She said.

"That *could* have been us," I said. It really should have been, it seemed right.

"And they were paying," Sela said.

"That's not important," I muttered. Too loudly.

Sela took her drink and threw it in my face.

I stood up, sopping wet. "What was that for?"

"You looked in need of a wash," Sela said. "So I thought I would help you out with my *fifth water*."

Lana tried to burrow into her cloak more. Yup, this was going to turn into something. I could feel glances cast our way, especially at the drips falling down my face.

Sela didn't seem insane right now. She wasn't referring to Sir Violet at all, which meant that this was her usual bitchiness rearing its ugly face.

"I understand that the days get hot."

"Hot?" Sela reached for her money pouch. "I wish it were hotter, it'd justify me throwing you in the damn river."

What was she talking about? So we were drinking water, we all were.

"But what I'd really like, at lunchtime, is something to eat."

Ah. That made more sense. We hadn't really done that eating thing for the last couple of days.

The bartender was casting glances in our direction. I really didn't want to get kicked out. Our room was above the taproom, and there had gone the last of our coins. We couldn't risk Lana to the mercy and tolerance of the streets.

No one, and not a single one of the books, really ever explained how you actually supported yourself being a superhero. Food just always seemed to be stocked. There was a bed to be slept in, and bills were more for work and a job. Quitting that job actually made being a superhero easier!

But now that doesn't seem to be real.

I stood up, and motioned Lana and Sela out. Time to let the bartender have his table back. And maybe think.

"Do you have a plan?" Sela asked.

"Working on it." I had been working on it ever since we stepped into Leftarch. We had done some good, really good stuff. We had foiled a mugging, stopped some goblins from harassing travelers, even broke up one of the bar fights two nights ago. That had earned us our last meal.

That was a thought. Muscle for the three of us. Stick together, we can get it cheap. Then by night…but muscle is needed mainly at night. No.

"Bank heist," Lana muttered.

"We are not robbing a bank!" I said. Seriously, that came out of Lana's mouth? I expected such a thought from Sela. Sela was practical to wondering why murdering someone wasn't an efficient way to get attention. But Lana was sweet, kind, comforting.

She pointed down the block.

"I meant there's a bank heist going on."

A bank heist? Now?

I pumped my fist. Finally! "Excellent! Let's go!" That probably wasn't the best thing to think. But this was going to be the most exciting thing we will have done. Real heroism, and we were right in the thick of it!

There were a couple banks in Leftarch, but the closest was Cerl's. Set right in the midst of the town square, just beyond the reach of the fountain and up their own marble steps. The columns stretched to a second story, it all was just so nice. It looked as classy as possible, holes in the plaster and thieves scattered about the front steps notwithstanding.

The thieves were all masked, pieces of cloth pulled over their mouths and noses. I knew it, that was what we needed to do, everybody does that in a pinch. A couple of dwarves, a human, an elf even, all led by a troll. Each of the five was armed either with sword or longbow, though the troll wielded a wand. They definitely knew what they were doing.

Lana pulled back her hood. "We're stopping them, right?"

I nodded. We were, somehow we were going to do that. There wasn't a militia here, and everyone was worried about the elves raiding. No one was coming to stop this but us.

Sela fingered the hilt of Sir Violet. "I suggest we kill them quickly, maybe enough strikes to cause quick bleeding," She always got less lucid when violence was imminent.

"Try and keep bloodshed to a minimum, Sela," I gripped my staff, and let the runes spark to life. "We're here to be heroes, not butchers."

Lana leaned against me. Eyes were wide, arms shivering, she couldn't contain herself. "We're going to have to fight."

"No," I hugged her close. "We, each of us, make the decision to fight, Lana. Never think it isn't a choice. If you don't want to, don't. Fade back, we will be back here."

Sela drew Sir Violet to full length. "They are getting away. I may die in horrible manner. Emelia would more likely survive."

This was not helping the situation. Lana looked up to me. I didn't know what else to say. Yes, please help us go do violence on strangers? No, be a young girl?

"How can I help?" She asked.

The Arch is truly an impressive structure. It stretches above the clouds, gracing us with a shadow that struck right across the square. I looked up at the buildings, and pulled the hood back up on Lana.

"Get up top," I said. "On my signal, you're going to fly down and scare them out of their wits."

"Because I'm ugly?" she almost had to pout.

"Because you scream louder than nine cats set ablaze," Sela said. Eeww, but yes.

Lana brightened at that, and latched to the building. Her claws tore into the soft plaster as she scaled up the side.

I shed my own green cloak as Sela dropped down to her duelist leathers. When I started out, I wanted flowing robes that gave an air of mystery. And a cape. After a week of traveling, I settled for a cloak when it got cold, but when we fought I wanted to be able to move. Witch or not didn't matter when the arrows started flying. A fashionable white blouse with brown leggings with a green belt was more than enough for style.

Sela was always prepared for battle. She had earned her duelist clothes in her first tournament, and since she acquired Sir Violet had yet to scratch her reinforced clothes. She still hadn't told me where she found such a blade. I don't know if she wanted me to know.

"Tell me," Sela drew Sir Violet, and looked down the purple blade. "Did you send Lana up so that she would never see a signal and stay out of the battle?"

"That is a terrible thing to say out loud," I turned around the corner and started towards the thieves.

"Because it's true?" Sela asked.

"Because she heard you," I called back. Two of the robbers looked at us, confused. Two girls, one armed and the other could be. One of the thieves, the elf, nocked an arrow and let it fly. Sela took two steps forward and sliced it out of the air.

She made her mark. Now it was my turn.

Concentrate. Let the magic flow within you. Let it build. Faster, stronger, just beyond your ability to control it. There, hold the reigns tight in your heart. Direct it towards the sky. Now let go.

My staff burst forth green light. It blinded everyone, the thieves crying out in surprise. The air ripped apart in a wave, sending everyone in the square flying. The fountain emptied in one blast of water.

The light fade out. My staff still smoked, green tendrils curling around my grip. I stared at the thieves, giving them my best menacing glare.

"You have something that doesn't belong to you."

They attacked.

That didn't seem right. No banter, no dialogue. Not even a wordless glance between the five to question just what two women were doing confronting them. Instead, the elf and human loosed arrows from their bows, and the other three charged ahead.

Sela spun out of the path of the arrows. She swept forward, Sir Violet meeting one of the dwarves' axe. Sela must have enjoyed the simplicity of this all. Nothing more than the fight and the kill. Sela was weird.

I fired another blast. The second dwarf caught it in the chest, spinning to the ground.

The troll looked at me, and pointed with a wand. "Kill the mage first," He growled. "She has power, but no martial prowess."

The elf and human looked at me, both raising bows. The elf loosed another arrow. Her partner charged, sword in hand. The troll and the dwarves focused on Sela.

Really, I was insulted. I sidestepped the projectile, twisted my hips, and slammed my staff into the side of the man. I actually did more than read in some dark corner. I worked out!

Not enough, though. The man grunted, but didn't crumble. He struck, and again. I parried once, ducked the other. Keep him in-between me and the elf. Step to the left, duck, what spell should I cast in this instance? I really needed to figure out a better hands-on spell. That's it!

The next blow that came hit my staff with the flat of the blade. I faked a grunt and let it fall. The man smiled in triumph. I lunged forward, arms outstretched to his face. I barked out a spell, and let sparks fly. Lightning coursed through my fingertips across his face. The swordsman spasmed in my grip, flying away to the ground. He lay there, twitching but alive.

I grabbed my staff and turned to the elf, expecting another arrow immediately after. None came. The elf was turned towards Sela, the archer's mouth open in shock and fury. Turning to Sela I saw why.

There was one of the dwarves, skewered on Sir Violet. The other dwarf and the troll stared at Sela, unsure of what to do next. She stared at her blade, almost questioning whether or not she did in fact kill her victim.

After a moment of pondering she pulled the blade out. Her victim slumped to the ground, and continued to bleed. Sela assumed a fighting stance. "Sir Violet told me that I'm allowed to kill at least one more person," She murmured. Sela pointed her blade at the troll. "You seem like the best choice."

The troll raised his wand. "I'm going to enjoy dissolving you," He said. The second dwarf stepped back, turned around and ran off.

"Coward," The elf muttered. Her eyes flicked back to me, and narrowed. "Don't even think about casting a spell. Skarg will melt your bitch friend if you so much as breathe wrong."

I turned my head between the three. The elf had an arrow trained on me. Skarg, I guess, had his wand on Sela. Sela, for her part, just stared at the troll. She promised death.

"Sheriff!" A voice called out.

I leaped to one side. An arrow passed through where my head was a second ago. I looked up to see the elf turn and run in the same direction as the dwarf had.

The troll barked a curse. His wand spat a yellow gel from its tip, almost reaching for Sela. Our duelist friend spun on one toe, the acid biting the air around her. She took a step forward, and spun again, another glob whizzing past her head.

Skarg the troll pivoted to match Sela's movements. They were in stalemate, until Sela miscalculated, or the troll ran out of energy to cast his spell. Or I stepped in.

I pointed my staff forward at him. A fireball could do it, might not even kill him...

Lana flew from the rooftop, screeching. Her voice scratched straight to my brain. I collapsed, screaming myself. Close the eyes, hands over my ears, let it cease. Lana would not stop. Her voice rang through my core, sending shivers down my spine.

And then it was done. I opened my eyes, and there was Lana. Standing right in front of me, staring at the man I had shocked. He was armed again, but confused. What was this creature right in front of him? And what was it doing?

He raised his sword to strike. Lana screeched again, oh no. it was even louder than last time! His sword clattered to the ground. Hands raised to his ears, he turned and sprinted away.

I curled up on the ground and just let myself fade away. Lana had stopped screeching, but my ears still throbbed. Was there bleeding? Hopefully not.

I felt a hand on my shoulder, pulling up. No, I shrugged closer together. Not right now. I wanted to just die for a while. It pulled back, insistent. Fine, I guess I was supposed to be around again. I sat up, leaned forward, and tried to get back to a conscious level.

A mustache looked at me. Thick, red, bristled. It was attached to a face that did not seem happy.

"What in the name of thirteen pantheons did you think you were doing?"

He was the sheriff. Without a doubt. He had the floppy hat, a battered dusted vest, weather-beaten leggings, shined silver boots, and an expression that promised vengeance.

And a badge. The badge is what really sealed it.

"Sheriff," I said. "Some of them got away, but we saw which way. Give us a second to breathe, and then…"

"What are you girls?" he asked. "And why do I have a slaughtered dwarf in front of the bank?"

Right. The dwarf. Sela stood next to her kill. She was cleaning Sir Violet, a vacant expression on her face. Did she know she had just killed someone? Or did she simply not care? This was getting out of hand.

"They were trying to rob the bank," I said.

"They?"

"Two dwarves," I grimaced. "One dwarf now, a man, an elf, and a troll…"

"With a wand," The sheriff finished. "One of the Arch gangs. Skarg, right?"

Skarg. Yes, that's what his name was. Somehow he had escaped Sela, something I hadn't thought possible.

"Skarg and his gang been running around for a while." The sheriff walked towards the bank. He raised a hand, and lowered it. "A bank heist, in the middle of the day…didn't think they were that open."

The sheriff nodded to the dwarf. "They'll be more careful. Or try to kill you."

"They tried," Sela murmured. "I persuaded them otherwise."

"Course." His hand trailed towards his vest. He probably had a few wands tucked away in pockets. Sela's eyes flicked down to his hand, and back up to his eyes. She'd skewer him on the spot, badge be damned. No, not on my watch.

"Sheriff," I cut in between them, hands raised. "You said they're one of the Arch gangs. That mean they have a hideout up there?"

"Could be," The sheriff nodded towards the structure. "Been crumbling for decades, filled with all types. Not dumb enough to go in myself.

"But you three," His eyes bored into my skull. Rage, absolute and foaming, all directed at me. "You three just run into a bank heist, determined to do what? Save the day?"

"We're heroes," Lana said. "We help people."

"The bank's insured," The sheriff muttered. "And they pay a good amount of my salary to make sure the scum is brought in."

"Not really doing your job then," Sela looked up at the Arch. "Are you?"

The sheriff tapped her on the shoulder. How... what? He had been a good thirty feet away, and unarmed. But he was there, a wand in hand and pointed at her throat.

Sela stared, surprise evident on her face. Sir Violet was in her hand, but hung useless at her side. If she so much as twitched the sheriff could end her.

"I'm working on it," The sheriff muttered. "Me. Not you three girls."

He nodded to me. "I want y'all out of my town by tonight. No excuses, no questions."

"We're trying to help!" I said. "We're trying to do good."

"The money is gone, and the only person you managed to stop is the one that now needs a burial." I almost collapsed at those words.

"You failed."

He was right. He was completely right.

The sheriff didn't arrest us. Said we weren't worth his time and energy. So that was a nice way to make us feel irrelevant. A real velvet way of kicking us out of town.

Sela and Lana watched as I packed our bags. There wasn't much left, not anymore. There would be less, I think. Some clothes that might be sold. That could get us another meal, two if we weren't too picky.

"Where to now?" Lana asked.

"I don't know, Lan," I said. "Maybe keep going west. There are bigger cities there. Or maybe even south, to the coast. There always seems to be work along the coast."

"But what about the gangs?"

"What about them?"

"Skarg is still out there," Sela said. "Him and his gang. They're just sitting there, counting their ill-gotten gains."

"That's right," I said. The bag was packed up. I lifted it up, tossed it over one shoulder. Not too bad.

"The sheriff is going to take care of it," I said. "We're getting out of here."

"Why?"

"Because the sheriff has a bunch of wands and a quick draw like you can't even match, Sela." Why was this so difficult? The duelist couldn't bother to pretend to care about anything else, only death and that dumb sword. We could do that anywhere.

"But they got away." Lana looked at the Arch. "We could maybe stop them and..."

"We're not heroes!" I screamed. "We're a bunch of girls that can't stop a bank heist."

I glared at Sela. "At least not without a body count."

"We killed before."

"When it was necessary, not just because it was convenient."

The duelist nodded. "I kill. I do, sir Violet does. There is a darkness within us, Mel. I don't want to stop killing people. We won't stop. With or without you we're going to..."

"Tpppbbtthhh!"

Lana glared up at the both of us. "Teenagers. Twenty somethings. So dark, so stupid. You're both just so dumb."

She grabbed my bag. Lana shook it once. "We save people. That's what we do. Because."

Her reasons were naïve. Her methods were crude and without any substance. Yet they made sense.

Sela looked up towards the Arch. "Sir Violet knows where they went."

Lana tossed the bag back on the bed.

"I want to be Batgirl."

We needed masks.

The Arch used to be a marvel to behold, so it was said. A gateway to new lands. But when magic came into the world, it grew, changed. Its old foundations, wherever they had been, faded into the landscape and growing towns.

Rumor has it that the Arch had once been small enough to be in one city. I doubt it. Leftarch alone holds over a thousand people in its walls, and can barely get out from the monolith's shadow.

That's what we were climbing up.

Hidden within the Arch, somewhere, was Skarg and his gang. Shouldn't be too hard? Even though it had grown, the Arch was still thin enough to jump from one side to the next. No real challenge to find them right?

The look on that troll's face when we went screaming into the cavern on top of the world was worth every scrape we got on the way up there.

The look was menacing, but that was a troll. He always looked menacing. With his jaw hanging open and eyes opened wide, he looked like he was ready to swallow me whole. But the small 'huhs' coming from his throat betrayed his surprise.

"How?"

Lana stepped forward, a black domino mask over her eyes. "Evildoers beware! Darkling has arrived!"

It was a compromise. As was Lady Violet. But I was the Green Witch, and there wasn't anything anyone was going to do about that!

"The Green Witch?"

And I was apparently thinking out loud. My staff was out, pointed straight at the elf. Sir Violet was within reach of Skarg. Darkling was giving her best menacing glare.

The gang, for their part, just stared ahead. A look of confusion was on everyone's faces. The elf spoke up, and pointed at me.

"You got here?"

"Apparently," Lady Violet (and yes, I had to think in their alter egos. Sela said she knew when I wasn't) said.

"But, the vampire rats," The man said.

"Scared of bats bigger than them," Darkling said.

"The caverns of mutated mushrooms."

"Nothing a simple spell could fix."

"And the giant dwarf city!" Skarg finally growled for himself.

Yes, they were all there. And more, far beyond anything I could have imagined. There was a world within that Arch, quite possibly literally. I couldn't believe we made it there in such fantastic time. But when Darkling led the way, we either talked it through, or flew. For some reason that just seemed to go faster.

The dwarf and man were not guarded. We were outnumbered, and I didn't like our chances to get out without bloodshed. Skarg started, and raised his wand up in the air.

"Question?" After I nodded, he smiled. "I guess you're here to kill us."

"Take you in to the sheriff," I clarified. "Killing is a last resort."

Lady Violet cleared her throat. "From them anyways. Resist enough and I get a free pass."

"Regardless, this seems a lot of work just for a simple bank heist," The dwarf asked. "For this effort you probably could've done some protection for the local barons, or even protected the bank from us in the first place."

"Doesn't matter," I said. "We're here now, and you're not getting away."

Skarg nodded. "No, we're not, are we?"

They didn't.

It's funny how battles go through your head, after they're done. The movements go so quickly that you forget that they had purpose. Some blows, or spells in my case, fade away while others are just burned so clearly into your head forever. I could run that entire fight over my mind, though granted it wasn't that long, with only the basic details hazy.

That was how we recounted it to the Sheriff afterwards. The money was dropped off at the bank, despite Sela's protests and even a half-hearted questioning by Lana. The bank would have known, and even if they didn't, we would.

The sheriff was in his nightshirt. Just seeing that mustache bristle above a fluffy cotton gown, it made me realize how tired we all were. Lana leaned against me, Sela clutched sir Violet a little harder, and we all just sank into ourselves for a last bit of strength.

Our awesome masks did not fool him for a bit. But he didn't ask what the heck we had been up to, or the ridiculous costumes we had on.

"Have you even had dinner?"

I tried to play it off. But Lana blurted out "not in a couple days," before I could beg off hospitality. Thank the gods for Lana's big mouth.

The sheriff moved to one side, and motioned us in. He sat us down at a table with a missing leg, and tore apart a loaf of bread. We tore into it. We had devoured the bread, a piece of jerky each, and tall glasses of water before anyone spoke again.

"So where have you been?"

Sela tried to look casual as she scanned the room for more food. "Top of the Arch, dealing with Skarg and his gang."

The sheriff laughed. "And how did that go?"

"Great," I said. "They're knocked out, all tied up by the bank, hanging and disarmed."

He stared at us for a while, not comprehending. We were going to have to get used to that.

"Why didn't you lead with that?"

"You didn't ask," Lana said. "And we didn't want to turn down such a great dinner."

The sheriff sat on his bed. He was pensive, and conflicted, all the more impressively done in nightwear. I finished down to the last crumb, downed the glass, and handed it to him.

"You're welcome," I said.

"I couldn't come close to Skarg," He murmured. "Those guys had a way up to the Arch, past all those traps and creatures. If I had a hundred men, I wouldn't have made that climb."

I shrugged. We all did.

"I could use deputies like you," he said. He rushed over to his nightstand, and started to rummage through it. "I swear I had some made, but with Skarg and the Arch scaring everyone half to death I wouldn't think..."

He threw his hands up. "I swear, there are deputy badges in this building. Or there will be, soon. And they're yours, if you want."

I smiled. Deputies. Paid, settled even. We'd be able to just eat for a while. Maybe need a job on the side, it wouldn't pay enough...and what would we do if the sheriff told us to ignore something a little too powerful, or connected? My mind went there in a heartbeat.

It must have showed on my face. The sheriff nodded. "They're there for you if you want them. Anything I can help you girls with?"

I nodded towards the Arch, and beyond. "Know what's going on west?"

He snorted. "Nothing worth your time. It's civilizing too quickly. The east is caught up in the Wastes or trading across the ocean. The north just wants to be left alone, and the south is caught up in too many messes."

"Southwest it is then." Civilized, chaotic. Maybe a hot meal on the way. Sela and Lana both agreed, and we stood up to make our goodbyes.

We left out the door, and the sheriff made his last attempt to stop us.

"Why are you doing this? No help, no pay, no gratitude. Why help people?"

"Because they need it." Sela said. She was right.

Proper War (or How Blood Feuds should never interrupt Dinner Plans)

On Thursday it was Mrs. Lana Milkshade's turn to host the monthly dinner party. It wasn't really, but poor Mrs. – excuse us, Ms. – Glory Nalus' house was the latest of recent conflagrations, and she simply did not have the necessary living room to host the event. Mrs. Milkshade's house also had a lovely view of the suburban areas where the elemental spirits were currently vying for control. The electricity and magma were mixing wonderfully with the pale yellow light of the air, especially in the mid-afternoon sun. So Mrs. Milkshade's seemed a lovely alternative.

Mrs. Milkshade believed her house was simply superior to the rest of the mothers in town. It wasn't because it was grandiose, not that at all. The grandiose houses were the first to go in this latest flare-up. Too many opportunities to detonate floors to rubble. It was instead a modest two-story affair of wood and stone, crafted by hand with the runes etched lovingly over the lattice to prevent evil spirits. Not extraordinary, but serviceable.

Rather, Mrs. Milkshade's house was superior because of her garden. The elm trees laced through oak branches wonderfully, forming a canopy over the stone walkway and giving the lilies some much needed shade. In the backyard stood one apple tree, unobtrusive in its pastoral grace. Mrs. Milkshade loved picking the apples and enjoying the shade of the trees that gave her such comfort. Some days she never left her walkway, drinking a glass of apple cider, freshly pressed, and enjoying the sights.

Some may ask where Mr. Milkshade was during all this. Mr. Milkshade had been a terrible bore for thirteen years before doing the world the good of removing himself from it, and Mrs. Milkshade was all the more content. She was happier as an old – that is to say, an older, being just turned forty-five – maid than she ever had been married.

The Mrs. remained. Mrs. was a title of respect and command, and she had earned it in Candid. She attended the monthly town meetings without fail, and was kind enough to only win first place at the annual flower competition once every three years. The people of Candid knew that Mrs. Milkshade was a Mrs. through and through.

Mrs. Milkshade was sitting on that same stone walkway, enjoying a cordial as Ms. Glory started to walk up the drive. Her clothes smelled of ash and sulfur, but otherwise she was not the worse for wear. She did not want to keep the Mrs., in fact had demanded that Candid called her by her maiden name. The scandal had remained in the town for a long while, however. Imagine, a good dwarf man like Gregus Battlesmasher, running around with some succubus with her whatever hanging out for the world to see. Mrs. Milkshade could only feel a pang of sorrow for poor Glory, and when this latest of tragedies afflicted her, had done the courtesy of ignoring it completely.

"Mrs. Milkshade," Glory said, standing on her tiptoes to peck the cheeks of the hostess. One showed proper respect to Mrs. Milkshade at all times. "I cannot tell you how grateful I am."

"Tut, tut, Glory," Mrs. Milkshade waved her hand towards a seat next to her. "It was my pleasure. How is Miss Wendt's abode?"

"Unscathed," Glory remarked. She looked down at the pitcher next to Mrs. Milkshade. "Would that be liquor?"

Mrs. Milkshade bit back a polite retort. Glory was settling back into single life, and was only two hundred. She wished to straddle flightiness and solidarity, a reed blowing in the wind whilst staying put. Allowances must be made.

"It is a lovely cherry cordial. Mrs. Eiri was kind enough to send some ahead of her for the dinner party."

"Which Mrs. Eiri?" Glory asked. She took the offered seat, being careful to move it just a few inches back.

That was a conundrum. The two Daughters of the Pale Morning never had the decency to take their husbands' names. Being a strong, independent woman was all well and good, but there was some inherent power in the sharing of a name in matrimony. Always take such power.

"Mereda," Mrs. Milkshade said. "And she is most likely fetching Mrs. Srie Eiri."

Glory nodded, sipping her cordial. She was thinking of the battle down the block. Currently the three O'Laney brothers were storming the Denton's house for strategic positioning. And the rumor was that Harold Denton had been stockpiling enough wine to end this war in a drunken stupor once and for all, if it didn't burn first.

Glory hoped the rumors were true. She was sleeping with Harold's son and two of the O'Laney brothers, and was hoping at least two of the warriors would survive. They were always so sweet to her, bringing gifts to her door and never once asking after her deadbeat husband, may he burn in the fires of perdition where he was most likely heading.

"Is that the Eiri sisters?" Mrs. Milkshade asked. They had not yet turned around the corner, but Glory had learned that Mrs. Milkshade never was wrong in what she heard. Sure enough, there they were, the Eiri sisters, different shades of pale. Mereda was always a slight dream of a girl, the last trace of night in her hair a black shock against a white mass of curls falling around her shoulders. Srie was brighter, pinks and orange eyes always peeking out of her rich tangle of blonde hair. They were not hand in hand, but the smiles on their faces would always describe them as sisters.

They looked seventeen, and had been for the last thirty years that Mrs. Milkshade had known them. She never knew whether the daughters of the Pale Morning was a religion, or perhaps more literal. She never asked, that would be too rude.

Srie nestled next to Glory, sitting on the stone walkway. She smiled, looking up. "Did you know that your house is just the most wonderful orange right now? Burnt, with flashes of scarlet. And the blue! The blue just is soft in the center. It is just..."

Mereda kicked her sister in the foot, looking up at Mrs. Milkshade in apology. "Srie, they don't want to know."

"Sorry," Srie said, not entirely understanding what she was apologizing for.

"May I have a cup of cordial?"

"Absolutely," Mrs. Milkshade said. "Your sister was kind enough to bring it beforehand."

"Thank you, Mereda," Srie said. She smiled, sitting down again.

Glory looked at the sisters as they settled in to watch. "Mrs. Milkshade, how are you this day?"

"I am doing quite well, Glory," Mrs. Milkshade remarked. "I was feeling quite peckish last night, but after a spot of beef, I felt right as the moon."

Glory nodded. "You have had no problems then with travelling?" Glory never was too polite to not ask about diet, but she did her best to put a polite mask over her words.

"Candid is always so kind when they see me out on my business," Mrs. Milkshade sipped the cherry cordial again. It truly was a tad too sweet, she preferred a touch of frost in the cherries before they were harvested. Gave the syrup a touch of night in the taste.

A bolt of lightning streaked towards the stone walkway, crashing right in front of the steps. Mrs. Milkshade arched an eyebrow, looking towards the source of the spell. A house across the street was being torn from its roots by a golem of magma. The inhabitants of the house were attempting to combat the beast with opposing elements, a deluge pouring out of the facilities while Francine Darlique let her staff gather energy for another blow.

Mrs. Milkshade cleared her throat.

The house stopped shaking. The golem, Francine Darlique and the inhabitants looked across the street. Mrs. Milkshade tapped her finger against the glass. Glory looked bored. Mereda rolled her eyes as Srie waved.

"Sorry, Mrs. Milkshade!" Francine called out. "We'll try and keep it down."

"Not a problem, Francine," Mrs. Milkshade said. "But if you could make sure that you do not hit my property. I fear for my poor lilies, they are not as strong as they used to be."

The golem burbled an apology.

"You're all doing great!" Srie shouted out. "Have a fun war!"

Glory stared at the two Mrs. Eiri. The daughters of Pale Morning were usually ready to burst in the front door, but now they sat, watching with interest for something they most likely did not know. Something was calling for them. Mrs. Milkshade apparently decided it was best to let it take its course.

"Mereda, I have heard that your husband is attempting to negotiate a peace." Glory took a sip of cordial.

"He was indeed," Mereda said. "A glorious negotiation between the families. The Darlique mages and the Servants of the Burning Earth,"

"Better known as Norri's brother's wife, Jane Yaspin, and everyone she managed to get to worship lava," Srie explained.

"And the Servants of the Burning Earth," Mereda continued. "Were going to sit down with the town council, and the committee set up by my husband,"

"Who is absolutely lovely, by the way." Glory wondered why Srie kept speaking. "Fredrick has been losing weight, and the fact that he was boiled this morning really has nothing to do with that."

Mrs. Milkshade frowned, and stared at Mereda. The Mrs. Eiri stared ahead, watching the golem cool across the street. If she smiled a bit as the lightning burst the obsidian into gravel, Mrs. Milkshade supposed it was permissible and not too impolite.

"Right, I would like to welcome you all into my home to a wonderful dinner party."

It really was a wonderful spread. Mrs. Milkshade prided herself on sparing no expense, no detail, all without sending out for a single pepper. The glasses were buffed herself, filled two-thirds with chilled water with a tea cup besides. Only one dish was cracked, the result of a particularly strong wind gust that blew through her kitchen before its caster realized their grave mistake. She reserved this for her own character. A spotless tablecloth, the candles remained unlit due to the early time, it

was all perfectly adequate.

Mrs. Milkshade watched as the ladies filed in, looking at the spread with renewed interest. She did not give herself the luxury of a sigh of relief, but a small crook of the mouth did suffice. Her friends, her guests, were here without fail, and at the appointed time with five minutes for polite conversation they were at the table.

She nodded to the new widow Eiri. There were arrangements to be made.

"Is there anything we can do, Mereda?" Glory Nalus asked.

"No," Mereda said. She took a drink of water, shaking her head. "Really, ladies, please do not bother yourselves. Fredrick most likely went the way he desired: screaming in agony for a path to peace."

"Ah," Srie said, holding a napkin up. "A legacy. We should all be so lucky."

"Seems frightfully dangerous," Ms. Nalus said. "Imagine if all of us went out there trying to be heroes."

"Glory, don't speak of such nonsense." Mrs. Milkshade poured a glass of tea for widow Eiri, then for her sister and finally Glory herself. "It is not for a polite society to be involved in such petty squabbles."

"Even if it is tearing the region apart." Mereda agreed.

"But don't we have a civic responsibility?" Glory pressed.

"To do what?" Mrs. Milkshade asked.

"To help Irene Olive." Srie said.

Irene Olive? Mrs. Milkshade vaguely remembered her. The slight half-elf newlywed. Lovely herbal beer, if in need of a hint of midnight ragweed. She lived several blocks up, closer to the forest. Why was Srie bringing up Irene Olive, she was not invited to the dinner party.

"She's hiding behind the apple tree."

Mrs. Milkshade's eye twitched before she stood up. Glory and Mereda were up and offering to help prepare the appetizers before she could even move towards the back door. The hostess thanked them and accepted the help. Poor Mereda needed something to do, and needed to not be alone. Mrs. Milkshade then turned towards the back door.

This was her place of residence. While there were visitors by every three days as polite society necessitated, they did not stay. There were no gentlemen callers, no salesman, and certainly no riff raff. She had worked diligently to keep her trees well maintained, and they helped mark her property off with both an open air and sense of ownership. And there was a certain boundary that one did not cross to keep Mrs. Milkshade in good graces. Mrs. Irene Olive had shattered it just now.

Mrs. Milkshade stepped out the backdoor, and surveyed for any damage. But despite an eye that could pick out a dandelion hiding in her fields of sunflowers, she could spot nothing out of place. The paths remained swept, there was not a flower bent, and even the elms on the other side of the property had all their twigs intact, which was quite remarkable given the lack of rain this month. It seemed like no one had been to the back to do anything but meticulous and spectacular gardening.

And yet there was Irene Olive's toe. Sticking out from behind the apple tree where she tried in vain to hide from Mrs. Milkshade. Barefoot, the poor woman must have run without even a slipper on her feet, which was just too much. And she was so considerate to the garden. Mrs. Milkshade closed her eyes, breathed, and smiled. It was a bit expressive for her, but given the war she was engulfed in, allowances were made.

"Mrs. Olive," Mrs. Milkshade began. "If you would prefer, Ms. Nalus and Mrs. Eiri are in the midst of preparing another spot for you for our little get-together. I would be delighted if you rested in a chair rather than my apple tree."

Mrs. Milkshade returned to the house, and sat down. She did her best not to fume, and the lovely cheese and crackers with tea provided by Ms. Nalus and widow Eiri were so much help. She did not see the ears poke out first from behind the tree, tipped with ash and soot. Nor did she see the torn green dress, and the blonde hair that had been hastily bound up to avoid the fires.

Mrs. Olive was never close to Mrs. Milkshade's level of sophistication. She let out a sigh, and a laugh, and a cry. She ran to the back door, being careful to keep the garden pristine. But she was elf enough that being proper was not a factor to field maintenance. It was simply a fact.

Mrs. Milkshade looked up as Irene Olive walked through the door. The quirk in her mouth returned. Perhaps with this she would fulfill her necessary good deeds for the week.

"Dear, try not to get ash on the set pieces, they are one of a kind." Mrs. Milkshade murmured. "Srie, would you be so kind as to help Irene find the facilities and some respectable clothes? I believe I have several dresses that have returned to fashion that I simply will not fit into."

"Thank you, Mrs. Milkshade." Irene said. "I cannot begin to express,"

"Facilities." Mrs. Milkshade took a sip of tea. "Now. We will wait, but not for long."

Irene Olive returned to see Glory involved in a raucous debate between herself, Mereda and Mrs. Milkshade. The dress remained the same – Mrs. Milkshade was perhaps a bit generous in believing she had ever been so slight – but it had been washed a dried with efficiency, as was the dear's hair.

"Much better, dear." Mrs. Milkshade said, motioning to an open seat. "You look positively lovely."

"I was going to say that!" Srie said. She jumped into a seat, looking on.

"What were you debating?"

"Involvement." Glory said. "Whether or not it would be proper to involve ourselves in this conflict."

"Which it isn't." Mrs. Milkshade said.

"But the possibilities…" Glory began.

"It isn't." Mrs. Milkshade said. "This is an internal blood feud that has to do with the Darliques and that insufferable woman up the block. The fact that they have amassed enough power to threaten the rest of the region is irrelevant. I will not be brought into this conflict simply because a Yaspin decided that this particular avatar deserved a war."

"What about the Darliques?" Glory asked.

"Francine Darlique is a very capable woman, which is why Jane Yaspin despises her." Mrs. Milkshade said. She stood up, absolutely furious. This was all well and good, and she was in need of a good debate to keep the blood flowing, but her meal was threatening to turn towards burnt!

"I will be back." She murmured. "Mrs. Olive, I do apologize in advance, I did not take any dietary restrictions of yours into account. I do hope you enjoy a pork tenderloin with a raspberry reduction and saffron."

"Did I also catch a hint of sweet potato for a dessert?" Irene asked.

Mrs. Milkshade stopped, and this time she did let a smile trace across her face. "Very good, Mrs. Olive. I added sweet potato to the crust of the tart to give it a hint of flavor."

Mrs. Milkshade watched the pork tenderloin as she lifted it out of the fire pit. It was not always this civilized. Hours slaving away in a kitchen, just to turn your head for one second and have it burn right through your fingers. But a constant flame from a hired spell was well worth every penny. As she did the cooking, Mrs. Milkshade believed she could consider this still homemade.

"What about Fredrick?" Glory asked. "What if it were Mrs. Milkshade's husband, or yours Srie?"

She continued, but Mrs. Milkshade was losing focus. Mr. Milkshade had done quite well being gone, as had Mr. Nalus. But Mr. Milkshade, that bore, that person who had tried in vain to make her not just respectable and polite but boring, she would not have it. She lived her life to the fullest, not through gallivanting off in sordid countries and even more sordid beds like Glory, but by being the best where she was. Right there in Candid, she was known. People knew not to cross her, without an inkling as to why.

Mrs. Milkshade had heard a nice boring tale. A woman comes up in nothing, in squalor. She is berated, belittled, made absolutely unknown for her entire childhood and much of her adult life. But she struggled and worked and suddenly she was pretty enough to catch the eye of the local princeling. Some foot binding rituals and a summoning circle to bind a fairy to her will, and soon the prince was falling in love with her over the size of her feet. She went on to live happily ever after in a palace that never made her stand up again. Apparently this is bliss.

Mrs. Milkshade picked up the tenderloin, and set it down on the dining room table. She engaged in small talk, her mind in several fascinating places. She was right in the dining room, engaging Irene in talking about the latest gossip on the war. Apparently someone had decided to involve the lower planes and summoned a demon to fight the Darliques, ("I bet you it was that no good Reginald Buxbottom!" Mereda said, finally losing her temper. "His mother never required him to wash before the community theater. Imagine summoning demons to a simple blood feud, what this town is coming to.") And it was currently navigating Main Street and the tripwires within.

But Mrs. Milkshade was also thinking on that silly tale. She would never use such a practical summoning on something as silly as a prince. She would never be allowed to tend a garden as a princess, let alone take the time to make a raspberry reduction. Instead she would have had that hapless fairy set to work on a wardrobe that was slimming, not appearing to be slimming, and then tackle the geology underneath the garden to remove some rocks before she tore a hand open. Sensible magic.

And still Mrs. Milkshade was checking on that tart. She was trying a new recipe, and didn't want it to disappoint. Her smile slipped. They would like it. Yes. Yes they would.

A man burst through the front door, sword and summoning stick in his hands. A blood-flecked beard covered a heavily scarred face, and he slumped to one knee. He was dressed in cloth and denim, torn and burnt.

Glory stood up, sticking her finger at the man. "Antonius Rascal Paxton!"

The man winced, and turned around. He put on his best apologetic face.

"How dare you come into Mrs. Lana Milkshade's house in such a state!" Glory exclaimed.

"Sorry, Glory." Antonius mumbled.

"Excuse me?"

"Sorry, Ms. Nalus." Antonius corrected.

Glory walked towards the soldier. "There is ash in your hair, your clothes are a mess, is that fresh blood on your sword?" It was not a question so much as a scream, as she had reached the young man and decided that the current decibel was not enough.

Antonius tried to make putting a sword behind his back as innocuous as possible.

"Don't do that." Glory chided. "You will drip on these carpets, and who is going to have to get the blood out of the carpet? Mrs. Milkshade?"

Antonius' eyes widened, and flickered to Mrs. Milkshade. Mrs. Milkshade drank her tea. This was not something she needed to be personally involved in yet. And a lady did not make threats in her own home. It was proper, and more effective, if another did it for her.

"What do you have to say to her?" Mereda asked.

Antonius scuffed his boot. Or rather, he was about to until he realized he might ground something into the carpet, and fear for his life saved him. "I'm sorry I dragged a blood feud into your home, Mrs. Milkshade."

"Apology accepted, young man." Mrs. Milkshade stood up. Antonius took a step back, hand gripping his sword. An eyebrow went up, as if something was both amusing and gauche to the hostess.

"Now, Antonius," Mrs. Milkshade smiled. "Would you like a piece of tart before you leave?"

"Yes, please." Antonius murmured.

"Then I believe Srie will be kind enough to pull that delightful confection out of the kitchen, and I would be happy to slice," She allowed herself just the slightest inflection on the *l* diphthong to watch the young man's stomach churn, "you a piece."

Antonius accepted the tart, and exclaimed that it was the most delectable piece of food that he had ever tasted, outside of his mother's. Exempting one's mother is acceptable and even required, though for all her skill in parenting, Mrs. Paxton truly could not bake to save her soul. This was actual fact. She lost it last week, thanks to that despicable Brenna Saxen's Flaming Jubilee, and was currently searching for someone else's soul.

While Mrs. Milkshade had to admit that her desserts would only rank seventh in the community bake sales (or higher, depending on the current death rate), she was pleased with the comment, and thanked the young man, who beat a hasty retreat out of the house and down the block towards the sounds of an ambush.

"Such a nice boy," Srie said. "Mrs. Paxton should be proud."

"Holds the sword with technique and conviction, and those manners!" Glory picked up some of the dishes with a smile in agreement. "Once he realized the error of his ways, he could not help but be polite."

"Fear will do that to a young man." Mereda pointed out.

Mrs. Milkshade waved her hand. "Tush and ravel, Mereda. The boy's fear has little to do with his manners. Manners are built into our bones. In fear we may ascribe to politeness, but it is only through practice and poise that it is achieved."

"And that is why there are too few men and too many boys," Glory called out from the kitchen. "Not enough practice!"

"Do we need to hold a ball?" Mereda asked. "We could bring it up at the supplication hearing next week."

The supplication hearing, oh dear. Mrs. Milkshade had completely forgotten about the premature planned surrender of the Darliques. This blood feud had been budgeted out months in advance on the social calendar, but already it was over budget. The Darliques were going to have to surrender early, or not even a production of Turner Vaughn Gnasp's immortal classic *Seven Spirits Sang Sweetly* could raise enough money to prevent a deficit. As if they could even provide the necessary sacrifices of gold and goblin secretions this late in the year to procure the necessary rights.

"We are already in over our heads with this silly blood feud." Mereda chided. "A ball would raise no revenue whatsoever."

"We could make it a ransom ball," Glory suggested. "Hold foreign dignitaries for funds. That would help us get back some of the funds from the war. And while they are here, they would instruct the young gentlemen in multicultural poise and elegance."

"And where would we get such dignitaries at this time of year?" Mereda demanded.

That was true. Most dignitaries of note had either already been ransomed this year, or were awaiting negotiations patiently. Several had been kidnapped by villages enough times to have contracted villas for their personal use. At taxpayer expense of course.

Mrs. Milkshade turned towards Mrs. Olive. She had remained almost silent throughout dinner, and even now seemed to want to shrink into the wood paneling. She was an uninvited guest, but a guest she was. Mrs. Milkshade would not have a disappearance in plain sight.

"Mrs. Olive, what do you think of this current town squabble?"

Mrs. Olive looked like she wanted to disappear as Mrs. Milkshade continued. "Or, perhaps you wish that we talked more of stopping the bloodshed rather than the social calendar."

The other ladies realized that Mrs. Olive had been entirely left out of the conversation. Glory reddened, while Mereda Eiri trailed off her in own thoughts. Srie Eiri leaned forward, suddenly very interested in what the woman had to say.

Mrs. Milkshade surmised that Mrs. Olive was quite typical for a half-elf. Irene Olive was not usually seen in town for a weekly dinner. Mrs. Milkshade doubted that this was an intentional snub. Half-elves were so often ostracized from polite society. Which was rather silly, when considered fully. There was an exotic quality to combining so diverse cultures as human and elf, or whatever else chose to breed with the elves.

"I just want the death to stop." Irene said.

Mrs. Milkshade nodded, and gathered herself up. "Come along, ladies." She made sure to pluck a hat off the rack, a nice little lavender shade that did accent her eyes so. Oh, and then the deep red with a wide brim for Mrs. Olive that just gave her a sense of life. Yes, that would make an impression.

"Please put this on, Mrs. Olive," Mrs. Milkshade moved around the house, checking a mental list of necessary tasks for closing the house for the dinner party.

The guests moved about, tidying up the house with speed. The Eiri sisters made sure the living room was spotless while Glory finished wiping down the kitchen. They had no idea just where they were going, or why. But Mrs. Milkshade was the hostess, and an outing was just the thing to burn off such a lovely dinner.

Mrs. Olive stood in the center of the four ladies, trying to be unobtrusive. Mrs. Milkshade placed her hand on the half-elf. "Irene, if you would be so kind as to make sure the back garden is still in good order, and then meet us on the front walk."

Mrs. Milkshade led the party out to the front door, and took one last look at the feud raging in the streets. It had been amusing while it lasted, but the war was starting to spill into her living room, and it obviously upset Mrs. Olive so. Even the new widow Eiri was putting on a brave face, and Mrs. Milkshade would not stand for that.

Still, the lava had always been such a relaxing sight while she had sipped an evening tea. And every once in a while a conjured flood did wonders for her garden. No, those were always interspersed with droughts that lasted for days. The weather was being used much too often as a weapon. It was time to end this.

Mrs. Milkshade stepped off her walk and nodded across the street. The battle had finally abated during dinner, and Francine Darlique and her boys were using the golem's body parts to prop up part of the house. She did have to admire the resourcefulness.

"Mrs. Milkshade!" Francine dropped her staff, bowing. "How was your dinner party?"

"Interrupted by Antonius Paxton." Mrs. Milkshade looked around. "Have you seen Jane Yaspin recently, or has her head been removed?"

"Jane is still puttering around the north end of town, holding it despite several tornadoes I sent her way." Francine grinned, and Mrs. Milkshade noticed a few molars were missing. When this was over, Mrs. Milkshade made a note to find a dentist that was travelling. They could make a fortune, and deprive some tooth fairies from nesting in town.

"I wonder if you would join me and my party in stopping this squabble." Mrs. Milkshade asked.

"But we were going to surrender next week," Francine began, and stopped when she noticed a tick in Mrs. Milkshade's mouth. "We didn't want to surrender early to Jane Yaspin."

"I have no intention of you surrendering at all, Francine." Irene finally showed on the walk. Mrs. Milkshade nodded to her, and started walking up the street. "I said we are stopping this. And I have no care of who declares victory."

That was a minor lie. Mrs. Milkshade was more than prepared to let Jane Yaspin squirm before giving her leave to surrender. This squabble was her fault, and it had upset her guests.

The walk through town was uneventful. The war being raged was fueled by passion and hostile differences that had no immediate answer. But the sight of Mrs. Milkshade caused the warriors to stop either to wave, or run towards a safer side of town.

Irene asked Mrs. Milkshade about this, and the hostess smiled. "The boys and girls know that I do not trifle lightly." If there was going to be any more explanation it would have to be subliminal.

As they approached Jane Yaspin's house, Srie stopped, and rolled her eyes. "Oh, tan sunrise!" She spat.

"Language, sister." Mereda said.

"Jane Yaspin is taking this too literally, Merey," Srie pointed, and the rest of the ladies did find themselves in agreement. Jane Yaspin had decided to raise a moat of lava around her two-story house. It bubbled and frothed, occasionally spouting up around the lone walkway towards the front door.

The burning rock was vibrant, and accentuated the obsidian walls nicely, casting a harsh glow that gave the impression of someone not to be messed with. Though it might have been more impressive if the Yaspins could raise enough obsidian to make more walls than a simple cottage. Presumably they still wanted visitors, but could not decide whether to be evil overlords of the melted stone, or prominent members of the community.

"You know why she did this," Glory cast her hand over the lava. "She never could get a single daffodil to take root."

Mrs. Milkshade whole-heartedly agreed, but let the others and Francine Darlique actually give voice to it. She was here for peace, not to comment on gardening choices, however misplaced their intentions were.

She stood at the foot of the walkway, ignoring the heat, and looked up to the window above the doorway. "Jane Yaspin, if you would be so kind and come out," She smiled as sweetly as possible. "We have a little war to discuss."

The window opened, and Jane Yaspin stuck her tiny little nose out. Speckled gray hair was cut close to her head, the ashes on her glasses seemed more a fashion statement than a result of hard work, and her portly figure did nothing but accentuate such. She stood there in a dress that flowed, actually flowed.

"Gods above and below," Glory muttered, "Is she actually trying to *wear* lava?"

"So it would seem." Mrs. Milkshade said.

Jane Yaspin leaned against the windowsill. "Lana," she drawled. "How nice to have you drop by."

Francine Darlique and the dinner partyers took a step back from Mrs. Milkshade. This was suddenly something that seemed hazardous to bystanders that came too close.

"Jane," Mrs. Milkshade said, looking up at the woman. "Come down here now."

"Or what?"

"Or I make you." Mrs. Milkshade smiled. "And then I would have enough regrets for us both."

Jane Yaspin seemed caught. She was in a role, a role she obviously loved. Queen of the melted stone, fighting a war that made the ladies in bake sales stand up and take notice. And she must have even thought she looked ravishing in that dress, though the effect might have waned in the last three decades she had spent in married life. The men would be the first to say they would rather jump in her moat than walk through the front door. She thought herself powerful.

But this was Mrs. Milkshade. And Jane Yaspin had already made the mistake of calling her by her first name. Jane disappeared from the window.

"Francine," Mrs. Milkshade plucked the hat from her head, and held it out to be grabbed by the Darlique. "If you would be so kind as to fetch two chairs."

Francine grabbed the hat, and frowned. "Two?"

"Afterwards, if you would be kind enough to console the newly minted widow Eiri," Mrs. Milkshade said, "and have one of your boys locate Mr. Olive. I am quite sure his wife would like to know if he survived the fire that obviously took their house."

Francine conjured two chairs, and started to hurry off.

"Francine."

She turned back to see Mrs. Milkshade, reclined in the chair and sipping from a tea cup that had appeared from nothingness.

"If I find that the widow Eiri is such because of your side of this squabble, I will call on you next. Doubly so if Mr. Olive is only partially located."

Francine bowed, and disappeared behind the dinner partyers.

Jane Yaspin's front door burst open as she strode forth from the walkway. The burning rock bubbled and geysered around her. It was rather impressive, if overdone.

She reclined in the chair, looking over Mrs. Milkshade with contempt. The hostess in turn enjoyed her cup of Shaeryan Jade. The lava did make reheating a non-issue.

"So you have sided with the Darliques." Jane sneered.

"I have sided with myself, Jane," Mrs. Milkshade explained. "As I always have done."

"Anything the Darliques have offered," Jane started, and stopped with a wave of the hostess' hand.

"The Darliques have offered me nothing, there is no ransom or leverage, and quite honestly there is nothing either of you have or have done that interests me personally." She took another sip of a tea. "But you two have upset my guests, so I would like this little squabble to stop now."

Yaspin leaned forward. "The Darliques are scheduled to surrender next week. Why not wait?"

"Surrendering next week will cost Candid," Mrs. Milkshade paused, summarizing the losses of the last few weeks and taking a calculation. "Sixteen houses, finally divert the river, make any land outside of my property infertile for the next three years, and make our reputation synonymous with quaint backwards hicks for two generations."

Mrs. Milkshade considered. "Ah, yes, and four dozen sons and daughters will have been killed. So rather the question is why don't you surrender now?"

"Me? Surrender?" Jane laughed. "I'm *winning*."

"No, you managed to slip the surrender into Mayor Brandt's monthly address, most likely through your niece engaging in entirely too crude tactics." The knowledge of such was given to Mrs. Milkshade by Tessa Marie Nancy, who always did gossip too much. "Francine Darlique was amenable to such because to challenge the mayor when he had been so kind in allowing your war seemed crass."

The lava servant was shaking violently. The geysers that had previously been for show now spurted onto the walkway and out of the moat, carving holes into the streets and surrounding foliage. Such a loss of control belied a lack of ladylike demeanor.

"I was content to sit this out as well. It truly was none of my affair." Mrs. Milkshade finished her tea. "But you truly are a petty little girl, and now I must step in, or I fear a month from now this house will be worshipping the stars as they fall from the sky on Candid."

Jane Yaspin remained silent.

"Send word of your surrender within the hour," Mrs. Milkshade stood up and turned to leave. "Or I will."

"Tell me," Jane Yaspin said. "Does being polite in all things forgive your absolute bitch tendencies?"

The lava froze, and retreated. Where bubbles and froth were a moment ago was solid rock. Rock that wished it could run. The house shuddered once, and collapsed in on itself. Jane Yaspin's own dress toppled her to the ground as it solidified into a block of obsidian.

Mrs. Milkshade turned to the little woman. "That was unwise."

Jane Yaspin scratched at the dress, to no avail. It had sealed her in as effectively as a tomb. Mrs. Milkshade tapped her foot against the dress. "If you had allied with a river, it might have made more fashion sense. But the rivers that could come to your beck and call know to fear me as well."

"Who are you?"

"I'm Mrs. Milkshade," the woman said, bending a gloved hand towards the little thing. "And I do not suffer slights."

The partygoers did not know what conspired next between Mrs. Milkshade and the once-proud Jane Yaspin. But she sent word of her surrender within the hour. Her forces conceded the bake sale to the Darliques as well as exclusive rights to the third-floor of the library. As that contained the spells on music, the Darliques were more than content and did not pursue the matter further.

Jane Yaspin was last seen skulking out of town in a cloud of ash. She most likely wanted it to be a cloud of promise, on vengeance and brighter days for herself and her kin. It mostly brought coughs and chuckles.

Mrs. Milkshade returned to her porch, and waited. Candid was becoming more exciting. There was talk of a carriage road. And after this year, they might even have a chance to kidnap their own official for ransom.

All was turning out nice and proper.

A Family Far Beneath the Stars

"Glorious Gnix, rat again?"

Gnaxley pointed his spoon at the young brat. "Eat your rat, boy. Your mother caught it this morning-"

"Last week."

"Last week, and preserved it just for you kids."

Gnaxley thought the rat was noxious. It had been pickled, and green flecks were breaking off the fur. He needed to be back on the raids or this would be a norm again. Where had he put the knives again? He only wanted Brench and Glaile using them to train. And then there would be beseeching the chieftain and great Nix to raid again and, oh no.

"Lyria, please stop picking through your food."

Lyria scratched her ears with a claw, looking up from the fire pit. Her amber eyes glittered with a small smile. "What, dear father?"

"Don't try and pull that. Keep eating."

"Yes, father."

Gnaxley held fast and pushed through another bite. Stupid example setting. Lyria stood up, wiping her face clean. "Well, thank you. All glory to Gnix for the food we have-"

"You're going outside again." Her mother murmured.

Gnaxley shoved a heaping spoonful of noxious rat into his mouth. The taste hit his nose and he started coughing, pushing away from the fire pit. The women looked at him, and he motioned to his throat before rushing to the underground stream that he'd diverted for clean water.

Gnaxley stuffed his face under the water, and exhaled. The earthy water filled his mouth, removing that bile that had rushed to his throat. He kept his face under the water, listening to the burbles and currents. Through them the muffled voices of his wife and daughter started to bicker.

The goblin sighed. His daughter Lyria was different. Goblins didn't go up above the caves and tunnels for fun. He went out on raids out of necessity, not pleasure. Too many races saw goblins as nuisances, or threats. Rising out of the caves was a risk for anyone, and worse. Who knows what she could bring back with her.

He pulled his head out of the water, and sat on the rock. Why did Lyria even want to go outside? It was so open, and empty. Nothingness filled every crevice, and the air rushed about in every which way. The light was blinding, there was no heat, and the creatures defied description. No, better to stay where it was safe.

Footsteps clattered off away from the fire pit. That would be Lyria, running rather than face another biting word from her mother. She was a lot like her father that way.

Gnaxley returned to the fire pit, to find his loving wife scowling in his direction.

"Run away again?" Gnaxley asked.

"Stupid, stupid whelp," Gnaxley's wife was a perfect goblin mother. Stern, demanding, unwilling to give an inch. If only Gnaxley was that way. He put too much on his wife. But she was the strong one.

"Are you going after her?"

"Yes, love." Gnaxley murmured.

"We can't keep protecting her. Something has to change," His wife turned to the rest of the rat, dumping it into the fire. Gnaxley moved away, turning his hooked nose away from the fumes. Who knows what could crawl into his lungs?

"Af-after the raid." Gnaxley promised.

"Better be true." His wife muttered. "We've already got three joys. I would not like a disappointment."

Gnaxley nodded, and moved away. He knew where Lyria was going.

Past the tunnels of the goblin tribe. Past the children, running through the streets with newly developed claws, or digging new tunnels deeper into the hills. Their adorable little scales were still gray and hadn't whitened, now furrowed together as they started their first real excavations in life. Other parents looked on with pride. That one would be a true miner, a true explorer. Places no goblin, no living thing had ever before gone. It was all below.

Past the pit. The tribe kept no guards. No sense in letting anyone know there was something worth guarding. Instead a narrow strip of rock a hundred yards long was laid bare over a cavern, no more than two feet wide. Any army that dared attack the tribe could be held off by a child armed with rocks. That is, if the child were brave. Braver than Gnaxley.

Start going up, up to the trails leading to the surface. He had been here before, though it had been months. The last raid had been very good, he had even killed a couple humans, earning him and his family food, and treasure. It had been enough to sustain them for a while, and he had never felt the need to return to the surface. Until now. And until the next raid. His family needed him.

It was night. Gnaxley and the rest of the goblins could feel what was night air and what was day air that found its way down the tunnels, and night air gave him more comfort. He could close his eyes and pretend he hadn't left the tunnels. But now he had to keep his eyes open. Lyria was outside.

She hadn't gone too far. She stood on the crags outside the cave, looking up. There was moonlight tonight, and she glowed. Gnaxley stood inside the cave, and smiled despite himself. Lyria's dark hair flowed down over her scaled face in waves, accenting a kind face. Her fangs were slight and did not show through a warm smile. And her eyes, eyes of amber, looked straight up in joy. She was beauteous. *Again,* Gnaxley thought, *despite me.*

"What do you see when you come out here?" Lyria asked.

Gnaxley sat on a rock in the cave, looking out. "Cold earth. Giant trees that want to fall. Rivers larger than the caverns and faster than rockslides."

"And looking up?" Lyria asked.

"Space. Too much space." Gnaxley regretted being so honest. He was supposed to be strong, he needed to be there for everyone.

"Space? Father," Gnaxley felt his arm being pulled, and before he realized it he was out in the open. Exposed, naked to the wind, he had to escape. But his daughter was there. Gnaxley calmed himself.

"Look at the stars. Father, look at the stars." Lyria whispered.

He looked up. There, beneath the ponderous moon, lay the stars. They lit and winked without rhyme or reason. They were there, lighting up the nothingness. Smaller than torchlight, with thrice the blinding glare.

"The stars fill the sky, a cavern of light above a pale sky," Lyria said. She walked forward, hands outstretched. "I want to touch the light. I want to sit in the glow, be in this world of comfort and warmth."

"And when it finds you dared to come out, how would it respond?"

Lyria turned to the cave, looking in.

"A goblin. A wretch, a thief, a grub in the dirt. That is what you are to them, Lyria. You're not a being, you're vermin. Something to kill and whet the appetite for a real challenge."

Gnaxley walked towards the cave, head hung low. "Stop stretching towards the stars. You will only burn.

"Come inside, dear."

The raid was set for tomorrow. Time moved differently up above than below, but Gnaxley was assured it would be night. Safer for the goblins who could see in the dark. The victims, no, the targets, would be asleep. They would die between breaths.

This was a human camp, a village on the outskirts of their species' territories. It was far away from the elves and their hated bows, or the other goblins and their staked claims. Gnaxley didn't have to ask if they ventured anywhere near the dwarves. No goblin wished to incur that wrath. Not yet.

Gnaxley stopped at a crevice, looking down and thinking. What was he forgetting? His loving wife? No, she had stopped loving him long ago. They slept on separate blankets, in different caverns if they could manage it. The children had been born long ago, and were now grown. There was no reason to keep up the pretense of romance.

As for the children, Gnaxley could not be more proud. His sons were much braver than he ever had been, and decisive. One of them, Glaile was already finding veins of precious metals and deep mushrooms below the caves. Some trades could establish relationships with outsiders, maybe even a permanent trade route. The goblins had been searching for some credence to the surface world for centuries, and his son had found it with his crew.

The others were good nuisances. One had apparently killed an elf. An elf! Gnaxley sat on a rock and recalled the story. The fool had dropped down a shaft, right in front of Brench. His son had been on the elf in an instant, knife already in hand and stabbing down before the elf even realized his leg was broken. Brench carried the hair out every now and again, just to show the naysayers that he was telling the truth.

They had all gotten a kick out of that tale when Brench showed up. He had been holding the head up high, asking what mushrooms go best with elf eyes. Adorable, and oh, how they all had laughed.

"Can't believe that pup came from a runt like Gnaxley," one of them said. Gnaxley couldn't agree more.

They were good boys, honors to Gnix.

Gnix! That's what he was forgetting. Gnaxley stood up, running through the tunnels. Forgetting to pray to his goddess, what could he be thinking? Gnix might be cruel. Or worse, she could be funny.

Gnix, trickster goddess of the goblins. She wasn't cruel, she wasn't kind. She was simply amusing to herself. She molded the goblins out of the crust of the earth, giving them scales for skin and long hair because it made no sense. She had gifted them fire, and weapons, occasionally even participated in battles. But she was gone in an instant, never satisfied to merely give satisfaction. Capricious to an art form.

Still, one did not wish to incur her wrath. Something as important as a raid demanded fealty and worship. She will be watching, to see who wished to strike off on his own luck. Just to make sure it turned.

Gnaxley turned the corner, rounding towards the altar. He would just say a quick prayer. Nothing that would make great Gnix take notice for either too pleading or not pleading enough. Just enough to be ignored.

"Great Gnix, watch over my father Gnaxley as he performs your work."

Gnaxley ground to a stop, just behind an outcropping of rock. Prayers were supposed to be private spectacles. Gnix loved pranks, or jokes, and sometimes participated in such on her own people. But when one of her followers asked for solemnity, she obeyed. And may the gods protect those who dared violate such an event.

Gnaxley shouldn't be here. But it was about him. As the subject of a prayer, he supposed he was meant to be there. Certainly he wasn't being smote down from above. He snuck a peek.

Lyria kneeled at the altar, eyes closed and hands clasped at her sides. Above her rose the altar. It was the best the goblins could manage, carved straight out of the cavern, an indentation in the wall that rose to the ceilings. Candles, real wax candles bought or stolen from above, lit the chamber, giving a soft glow that Gnix found comforting. Her image filled the chamber, either laughing, or shouting, or jumping for joy in any pose around the room. She was given form in statues, paintings, there was even a wood carving leaning against a wall. Goblins were given to finding their goddess everywhere, and usually took their goddess back with them unless it was bolted down. And if they happened to have the proper tools, not even then.

The only feature that distinguished Gnix in all her forms was her smile. A half-smile, the right corner of her mouth was always turned up. There was always something the goddess found funny, even in the depths of her wrath. Possibly because she found her own rage humorous.

"Gnaxley was given your name to honor you, great Trickster. Protect your descendant, even from his own folly."

Gnaxley kneeled down, listening in.

"I love my father, Gnix. Even if he doesn't wish me to love my life, he cares. He fights on, in fear and doubt and sadness, he fights on. Let him find his joy. Let him find his peace."

"She gives a good speech," Gnix murmured.

Gnaxley nodded.

"In fact, that is the most eloquent that particular altar has ever waxed since those candles were placed there a century ago." The goddess said. "I should know, since I made sure your grandfather wasn't stung too much when he pilfered that bee temple."

Gnaxley stopped. He didn't know if his complexion could turn any paler, given its natural pigment. But he gave it a true attempt as he faced his goddess.

The goddess of the goblins looked blue. A blue glow shined off her scales, deep and low to bask in her beauty rather than blind it. She was dressed in a red dress cut off at the thigh to move around the cavern. There was dirt all along her very fine legs. Even the way her claws scraped along the cavern wall was a melody to Gnaxley's ears.

"Look up, Gnaxley. You're staring wrong."

Gnaxley snapped up to look into the yellow eyes. Gnix smiled.

"There's that wonder and fear."

"Gr-gr-great Gnix," Gnaxley stammered. He should be bowing. No, kneeling. Prostrate on the ground? Which would she prefer?

"Oh, dear Gnaxley," Gnix said, brightening her hue. "I've missed your mind. It stammers even when it thinks. Come here and give your goddess a hug."

Gnaxley rushed his goddess, hugging her. She was cool, and enclosed him in her arms. Suddenly everything poured out of him. He hated his life, his wife. She was mean to him, who makes their own husband lick their claws clean before he eats rat? And her rats were disgusting, you're supposed to use a deeper mushroom and the stem. And burn the darn stem with the rat, it clears away the fur and the char accentuates the stem's own flavor. How hard is rat?

And his kids. They always laughed at him, never cleaned the house, except for Lyria. All he wanted to do was be alive and safe and not have to go on raids.

Gnaxley spasmed as his sides were suddenly prickled with claws. A new sensation was there, and a claw clamped over his mouth. He started screaming out, muffled tears pouring down his eyes as his goddess tickled him mercilessly. Gnix held him close, her smirk shining as her fingers trailed across his sides. Gnaxley started laughing, coughs being worked through.

Tickling. He was prostrate on the ground, and in the embrace of his goddess she felt that his heart needed a good raking of gentle claws. There may have been more powerful goddesses, and gods that moved the heavens and the earth with impunity, but truly there were none such as Gnix. Only she understood a goblin and its lovely malice.

After an eternity Gnix released him. He laid on the ground, wheezing as air finally returned to his lungs. Gnix looked away towards the altar.

"You've been holding that rambling far too long. Your thoughts are far too ordered and meek, Gnaxley. You need to straighten them out."

Lyria stayed at the altar. If she had heard anything, there was no sign. Gnix smiled, warmly this time. "That one, she has her thoughts straight. It's her body that is wrong. I'd change it if I could, but she is quite content to be where she is, miserable."

"What," Gnaxley took a deep breath, composing himself. "What about her stars?"

"She'll grow out of them." Gnix said. "In time. She just needs to recognize that truth."

"Why?" Gnaxley asked.

"Because I want her safe," Gnix said. "And I can't be there all the time. She needs protection, you all need my protection. You'd all have been wiped out centuries ago if it weren't for my intervention. I need to watch over all my people. If some girl wants to run away from the flock and look at lights in the sky, she has to take her risks."

"So she either dies outside," Gnaxley said. "Or inside."

"Death," Gnix let her fingers trail through the haze of flame, "is change, Gnaxley. Change is all we are rushing towards. Goblins especially. There is always something different. Not more, not less, but different. It is when we get caught up in the sameness of it all that problems arise."

"She's going to be less because of me." Gnaxley said.

"It's her choice. Her prayers are for you."

Gnaxley stood up. "Her prayers are for my joy."

Gnix's smirk returned. "You always were smarter than you were told."

"Gnix, please give her the safety to carry out her dreams. Let my daughter have the opportunity to be who she wishes to be."

"Be careful, Gnaxley." Gnix stood, and suddenly she was larger than the cavern. Gnaxley took a step back. "You ask what you do not understand. There will be consequences, both for you and your family. Are you willing to accept this so your daughter can twirl through the night? Are you willing to be changed?"

"Yes."

Gnix smiled, and spat in her hand. She stuck it out to Gnaxley. "Deal."

They clasped claws.

Lyria disappeared just before the raid.

Gnaxley hefted his sword, shaking his head. He understood why she had done it. Everyone was busy preparing, too busy to watch for a little girl with her head in the clouds. But he had noticed the pack that had been bulging underneath her cot. And the practiced scratchings of a map. The drips of a hastily drawn water skin that led towards the upper caves.

No one paid much attention to her absence. Lyria was smart, determined, independent, and happy. His wife had considered shoving Lyria down a shaft to hide the shame and save everyone the trouble. When Gnaxley got back he considered throwing some mud in his wife's face. Or something stronger.

Figures. Even in his fantasies he couldn't imagine killing his wife. Gnaxley truly was a coward.

He chased after the rest of the raiders. They were all experienced, but always in need of more hands. The more you took, the more you kept. Kills were rewarded, as well as keeping a portion of the meat. A good raid could feed a family for a month. For three if you season the meat right. Six if you didn't care if it went rancid.

Everyone was considered expendable. Each goblin knew the risks.

Gnaxley looked at the village. Filled with loggers, taking trees by the root to clear more land to inhabit. They made their own clearing, but there was no wall. Good, and all the lights were off to boot. Simple dash in and kill anything that moved.

The raiders stood at the edge of the clearing for a moment. Then Brench howled, running forward. The rest of the horde soon followed.

The lights flared alive, and a man stepped out of one of the outlying houses, staff in hand. No, no they couldn't have a sorcerer. They couldn't afford a sorcerer.

Gnaxley knew that there were these legends called heroes. They were savage killers, allied to those of moral superiority with enough coin and comfort to have morals. They had access to power that rightfully remained with the gods. Like this person. It couldn't be a sorcerer. The villagers couldn't have raised enough money.

Lightning flashed on a cloudless night, alighting on his staff. Yup, that was a sorcerer. They were all going to die.

Gnaxley watched as the lightning sped through Brench's chest. His precious elf hair burned with the rest of him, and the five raiders behind him. The rest of the horde scattered. Some continued their charge, even as the humans started to pour out of their houses, armed and ready. A few with a sense of self-preservation turned tail and fled, pierced by arrows and lightning bolts alike.

Gnaxley stood still and looked up. The stars were out, as well as a waxing moon. It shone down on the humans already bearing down him. Around him goblins jostled him in every direction, but the moon stood still, looking down at him.

A flicker of a shadow traced across the moon. Was it a smirk?

Nope. That was an arrow. Coming straight at him.

Lyria shivered, huddling further into her cloak. The outside world was both warmer and colder than she ever could have believed. She had only ever tried to scale the hills to the crest. Going down left her feeling exposed, and open. It was wonderful, and terrifying.

There had been a lightning flash earlier. Lyria wept a tear in its direction, knowing that the raiders were supposedly in that direction. If it had been any magic, she might be without some brothers. Or worse, an orphan.

Lyria had wished to say goodbye to her father. But to face him, to look him in the eye and say that she was never to return, was unbearable. She would not have been able to leave. So instead she sat in underbrush, waiting for the cold to subside so she could continue to the river. From there she would find a town. A friendly town.

A friendly town to goblins. Was there even a place? Lyria knew the odds. If need be, she would live on the outskirts. Make the outside world respect her, if not like her. Great Gnix, she was a little girl.

Lyria stopped thinking and concentrated. Get down off the hills. Get out of the goblin territory into her unknown. Be warm, welcoming, and ready to run. Always be wary of offered help, and never look down on offered work. *Nothing is beneath me.*

There is always a joke to be found in a dark world. That was her favored saying of great Gnix. No matter the peril, no matter the sorrow, there will be a laugh to be found.

Footsteps sounded above her. Lyria stiffened, and snuck a peek through the brush. Up above, looking through the hills, were three human males. They were dressed warmly, and well-armed. One of them bore a staff, looking around questioningly.

"I still don't understand why your village insisted on hunting down any stragglers." The staff wielder muttered. "Those goblins that survived will never return."

"Says you." Another male said. "But what if they seek vengeance?"

"Goblins?" The other man laughed. "They're not concerned with vengeance. This raid wasn't personal. They were just hungry."

"And wanted to make a meal out of me and mine," The second man shot back, kicking at the mountain. "We hired you to take care of our problems, sorcerer. Are you planning on abandoning us now?"

The sorcerer stood still, and Lyria almost shuddered at the man's expression. "Every one of the souls in your sad little village is safe because of me. I have performed exactly as the contract bade. If you want me to start taking out entire goblin villages and running a one-man war, think again. Ten villages your size could not scrape enough coin together."

The sorcerer turned away from the second man, turning away from the trail. The second man kicked again, and threw his sword in frustration. It tumbled over and over, to land in the bushes next to Lyria.

The man scowled, starting after the blade. Lyria almost screamed, grabbing at the weapon. She was never good at fighting. But sticking the end into the other person was the idea. What if she couldn't?

The hills rumbled, rocks starting to fall. The sorcerer turned back, looking down. "Man, get down!"

"That's my sword!" The second shouted.

"That's a rockslide." The sorcerer said, pointing up. Sure enough, the stones had begun to roll down the hills. One bounced, just whizzing over the brush Lyria laid in.

The man ducked, and cursed. He started to move towards the brush again, and a boulder rolled past him. He turned and fled, shouting at the sorcerer already fleeing down the other side of the mountain.

Lyria lay for a moment in the brush, clutching the sword like a stuffed animal. When she could hear no more stones, she looked up. The sky was still clear, though the hillside itself was a mess. Turf was pulled up and strewn across the path, and a fresh pile of rubble lay at the bottom, nestled between a sturdy copse of trees.

Lyria could see the two men walking down the path, the second one still cursing.

"Lousy rockslide. I was certain we almost had an entrance discovered."

A branch caught his trousers, tearing a hole along his rear.

The two stopped, looking at the new hole. The sorcerer laughed. "We have indeed!"

The other man started to kick again, then thought better of it, and simply folded his hands behind him, trudging towards town. The sorcerer followed, giggles escaping from him every few minutes.

Lyria smirked, and turned the other direction. She knew the river curved a little bit. Once she got on the other side, there'd be no sign of her or the goblins. Everyone would be safe.

She hoped Gnaxley was safe. She had prayed for it.

Gnaxley watched as his daughter walked down the hills. She looked more confident than when he usually saw her. Relaxed in her surety. The night air, cold though it was, was doing some good. Not that he felt it. He didn't really feel anything.

He looked back at his hands, wondering how they moved. The wisps followed right behind where he thought his hands were, making his movements seem slower, languid. If he concentrated, the trails of smoke stopped. But it made his movements seem jerked, sudden. He'd discover a happy medium.

He was happy that he could still function as a ghost. He wasn't able to affect the living souls, but that tree only needed a slight encouragement to tear along the man's trousers. And the rocks were almost already set in place for a tumble. Gnaxley didn't want to question good fortune too much.

He was losing sight of Lyria. Gnaxley started moving, a smirk back on his face. He'd find a way to make her laugh soon.

There was bound to be some humor in this wide world.

The Ax Rises

"Well, ladies and gents, the final match of the Ionian Cup is just about to get underway. Tauren against the Sun, ARE YOU READY FOR SCRAMCRASH?"

This was truly living. Hear the roar of thirty thousand strong. Think of how many more are watching the projections back home. Let their screams pump through your veins. Feel it in your chest, your soul. Let their fire fuel your own. Time to take the field.

"And there is Ax and the rest of the Cretan Taurs. A fantastic season, led the league in scoring and total health of their Vortex. That bullrush, pardon the pun, is dare I say unstoppable."

"Unstoppable. Ha." Thesia removed her helmet to shake the sweat from her hair. It glinted gold in the sun. A bright day was necessary for a Sun victory, and the gods were kind enough to grant her such. The Athenians would be the ones who would carry the day into tomorrow.

"This is Corralee Muncie, your commentator for this prestigious match. As both Crete and Athens take the field, I can report that the stadium is filled to way past capacity. There are flyers, diggers, and many are just hanging onto the pavilion for dear life. Once in a lifetime opportunity, folks. To say you were there.

"The real story here, and I have no qualms about confirming it, is we have several scouts here from the prestigious Superior League. Five years old, and already the contenders are surging to the league for the honor of playing the best. And while both Crete and Athens would hope for their entire team to be invited, we all know the scouts are just here for one of these two."

Me. They're here for me. Ax looked up towards the stadium. The fans were screaming, rabid. It was still fifteen minutes to game time, they didn't care. They were witnessing their hero.

Surdiax, or Ax to them, felt uncomfortable. Runners weren't usually the center of attention. It was the Vortex that were both on the field and casting spells. The Slingers were sexier, with magic roaring from fingertips. Even if they couldn't set foot on the field, they were majestic.

Majestic. Power. Sexy. None of these easily described Ax. He was chunky, arms like blocks with digits that were bigger than an elf's forearm. His horns curled down instead of an alluring up. Ax even figured out how to best consider his snout disfigured.

None of these people cared. They wanted him. Needed him. Hated him, because he could do what none of them could. Shut that pretentious little elf's mouth by chucking a ball harder and faster than anyone else in Ionia.

"And there's the Athenian team. Thesia's runners clearly favor speed over strength, with centaur Ruk and the Valkyrie sisters." The Valkyrie sisters. Recruited from the frozen Norland, Thesia had lobbied heavily for them. The sisters Ala and Gegrun had responded with ten points apiece, and in an eight-game season no less.

Ruk was a mystery. More support for the women, he was one of the original members of the Sun a decade ago. Losing a step had wreaked havoc on his popularity, but his speed still outmatched most of the Ionian league.

Ruk wasn't even his real name. It was Orukus. Ruk seemed fiercer to the fans. He didn't have the heart to correct them.

Ax focused on the slingers. Thesia had kept around the dryad Iris, to have at least two players that could claim Athens as a genuine home. She was good, and even in Crete there was enough of a forest on the field for her to play with.

The real danger was Thesia's handpicked girls from the Black Forest. Meira and Naevys had some of the fastest draws that had been seen, and they played fierce. Most runners didn't walk away from the field without at least one broken bone. If they caught sight of Ax, he wasn't getting off easily.

He grinned. Sef and Not would have their hands full.

"Thesia and the rest of the Sun is a handful, but if there's anyone who can topple them from the heights, it is this Cretan team, playing for their home crowd! Jonah, Norie, Airelle, Fewdor, Sef, Not....aaaaannnnnnnnnnddddd AX!"

The press was a bit embarrassing for Ax. But the scouts were watching because of it. There were fans screaming his name because of it.

Stop it, he thought. *Focus on the match, on the team. Scouts hate showoffs almost as much as they despise losers.*

Lose the match, and no one would care about him. Ax would be the loser, the afterthought. At best, or worst, he'll be propped up to make Thesia look more impressive.

Ax fell forward. Sef reached a hand forward, catching Ax before the fall was anything more than a believable stumble. "Thoughts here, Ax," The satyr murmured. "Don't let 'em see you sweat."

Of course. That was it. Already the elves were watching them, waiting for a slip-up. The Valkyries and Ruk were examining equipment, the Dryad admiring the trees. The elves only had eyes for Ax.

Fewdor stepped up to the line. He stood eighteen feet tall, looking closer to twenty under all the muscle mass and gruffly groomed mustache. He, like Jonah and Ax, actually decided to wear full clothing, a dark crimson tunic to represent the Cretan team with full pants that severely cut into the team's budget to produce. However, it was a stipulation in his contract to have pants, a true treasure for giants.

Airelle and Norie perched on each shoulder, and glared ahead. They wore sashes across their breasts, more for sake of propriety than preference. Their talons dug into Fewdor's flesh, but the giant didn't seem to mind. Instead, his clenched fists almost seemed pointed at the Athenians.

"Thinking I might want harder pillows, Ax," the giant rumbled. "Or just toss a few boulders again."

"No boulders," Jonah said. Jonah Reeves knew he wasn't the captain, but he had to put his foot down. The rules were limited in ScramCrash, but the clearest was no lethal damage. A giant throwing rocks bigger than their targets might break more than just some bones, and send the entire team packing.

Not scowled, and leaned closer to the rest of the Bulls. "Sef and I've been doing our readings, Ax," He said. The satyr nodded towards the team. "The Valkyries are fine, but the elves play *mean*. Knocked out the last team, and saved the Vortex until the rest of the team was unconscious."

Ax had heard. He'd heard a lot worse of Thesia. The elf was determined to make the new League, and wanted to prove that not only was she the best, but so much better than this little league that dominance was commonplace for her.

It was something Ax desired too. This new League was amazing, a true chance to compete against the best. But the cost of Thesia's methods just turned his stomach.

"We're not devolving into playing their game," He muttered. He nodded to Thesia, who glared right through him, looking for weakness.

"We play our way, and when the whistle blows we'll have our heads held high with pride."

Jonah nodded, and started to give the finer details to the rest of the Bulls. Ax closed his eyes, and walked towards the center of the field. He liked to have a feel for the dirt before the ball was thrown. A little bumpy today, cracked. The earth was a little parched, no rain for a while. There will be a dust kick-up, might hurt the Slingers' accuracy.

"You are a mystery, Ax."

He looked up. Standing a hundred feet away was Thesia. She was looking at a tree, and placed a hand on it.

"Olive," Thesia said. "We don't have these back north."

"I'm not a mystery," Ax said.

"You are," Thesia said. "A minotaur with no herd to call his own, almost insisting upon it. Most of the beasts are wearing their history upon their chest or horns with pride. You leave yours bare."

Ax remained silent. He didn't like to talk about his past. He preferred to leave it behind. And too many questions would just lead to more.

"No response? Or just too hard in the head?"

"Are we going to talk, or play some ball?"

The announcer's voice reigned. "Looks like after some tough words from the captains, the teams are ready, let's take you to the center of the field. There's no tradition with the Bulls, once again Ax will be joining Thesia for the toss.

"The Sage today is one Maraelyn Bax, having watched over 346 ScramCrash matches. An air Elementalist by trade, we should be looking at a traditional cyclone to start the match. As we settle in for a fantastic match, I'd like to just remind everyone that to stay safe, and by hearing this you have accepted the angers of this match. Don't die from an errant spell or boulder, you'll bring the mood down."

A wind started to blow through. Thesia did not bother looking for the Sage, Bax was notorious for wanting to stay out of the spotlight. The spectators would know where he was. All he had to do was count her points, and stay out of the way.

A glint of fading light appeared a few feet in the air. The orb! Time to play.

"And Thesia takes the ball and the Athenians are off! We're seeing some archery right now, Sef and Not can't come close to support. The Valkyries are blocking Ax and…is that a pillow?"

Finally, Fewdor was finding the field.

"Pow! Right in the face! Thesia is stunned, and her Runners are distracted."

Distracted? Everyone was distracted. The Bulls never bothered with a cohesive strategy, just roles that everyone needed to fill. However, this was more chaotic than any of the players were used to. The Runners had all scattered, running for cover. The Slingers from both teams were frightfully accurate in the open field, be it by bow, spell or pillow.

Thesia dodged another of the projectiles, this one the size of a crate, and did a quick head count. Ruk and the Valkyries were fighting Ax, while the Satyrs had taken for the trees, sprinting away from Meira and Naevys' arrows.

Thesia spun again, and grit her teeth. The damn giant was ignorant beyond belief, but he was accurate. She slid next to a tree, and called up a communications spell. She breathed the words, and the Sun could hear her commands.

Straighten up! We're the Sun, not a damn apprenticeship. She almost screamed through the spell. *Iris, move the trees into something resembling order, give the rest of us some sight lines!*

These trees are foreign. Iris protested. *They aren't used to me.*

I don't care! We need to find people, and now.

The team snuck glances her way in combat, unused to such ire from their Captain.

She opened her arms wide, showing her entire body before disappearing into the trees.

Who has the ball?

This was not going to Ax's plan. This wasn't even close to what was supposed to be the plan. He blocked a swing from a blunted spear, and lashed out at the Valkyrie. His fist crumpled the armor, bruising both his hand and her side. She grunted, and swung again. Ax could respect that.

"Ball's gone!" Sef called out before disappearing again. No arrows coming his way, though there were rumblings from the trees. Dryad was going to find some trouble on their home turf. The trees knew Ax's team, trusted them. And the archers had to focus on Sef and Not, in case they had the ball.

But where was it?

Ax adjusted his stance, and kicked out. Unlike most minotaurs with manlike feet, Ax's body ended in solid hooves. When he kicked out right, armor wasn't an issue.

"And Naevys goes down! Ladies and gents, this here is a match! We've got spells being thrown by the harpy sisters to bog down Ruk and Thesia. The archers are trying their damndest to pin down Sef and Not. But of course Ax is proving more than enough for the Valkyries..."

BONG! A horn blew through the stadium, and the crowd erupted into cheers.

"Crete scores! Crete scores! I have no clue how but...there's Reeves!"

There he was, crouched next to the glowing sphere. The ball spun in the center of the energy. The Vortex was sucking in his breath harder than normal, but was all smiles.

"That would be Jonah Reeve's first point *this season.* A defensive Vortex, he's usually found on the outskirts of the field, communicating everything. But here in the Championship he just up and fools everybody, gods above and below..."

You said it. Reeves winked at Ax on his way back to their side of the field.

"You had one job," Ax muttered. Reeves laughed.

"I stayed safe. And I kept something to keep me company."

"Stayed safe?" Ax nodded to Thesia. She was screaming at the entire team. Heat broiled off her. Iris shuddered away, and even the elves looked nervous.

Thesia looked at Jonah with pure venom. He paled, and took a nonchalant step behind Ax.

"You just pissed her off."

"If you don't mind," Reeves whispered. "I'm going to try my best to disappear for good for the rest of the match."

"Sure thing."

Reeves was often criticized for his play style. His method of illusions and defensive spell weren't in the spirit of ScramCrash, ran contrary to its aggressive nature. But if a Vortex fell unconscious for any reason, the match was over. He was an integral part of the team, and his presence was irreplaceable. Ax and the rest of the team wasn't going to risk him over something as silly as tradition.

Sef and Not appeared next to Ax. "What do we do now, Ax?" They asked. "Run interference?"

Ax shook his head. "Just play our game. This isn't close to over."

It wasn't. Whether Thesia's criticisms were heated, they focused the Sun team. Thesia fell back into a support role, able to utilize magic up close while protected by the Valkyries. With her running havoc through the Bulls, Ruk was able to gallop past the team and tie the match up.

Ax felt a bit of rage. Ruk was his man on that exchange, and he was just beat out for the ball. Maybe that was why his punch broke Ruk's nose as he ran past the centaur to score again. He needed to work on that response.

The scores started getting faster and faster. Thesia scored once, then again. Ax repeated, then Sef. Then Not and even Fewdor managed to bank the ball in off one of his throws. They started to pull away.

The Bulls were finding a rhythm to the elf that was making it easier to predict. Thesia needed to have the ball on every possession, to the point of insanity. She would break through protections and expose herself just for the chance to appear before the scouts. It was getting too easy.

Then Thesia disappeared.

"Bulls are up by three, and don't seem to be letting up anytime soon. We're thirty minutes from regulation and...where did the Sun captain disappear to?"

Ax's head snapped up. Sure enough, Thesia was nowhere to be seen. Sef and Not were playing keep away from Ruk, avoiding the centaur's legs as the harpies and Fewdor ran interference. The Valkyries were there in the thick of it, but the Vortex...

Oh, no.

"And Ax is gone! The two captains have completely abandoned the ball, what is going on? Wait, there, there! At the Cretan goal is Thesia, dueling Reeves. Oh, this is a classic mismatch, ladies and gentlemen. Reeves may be good at evasion and illusion, but he is simply outclassed. But why?"

Why indeed. Thesia was throwing fire, lightning, pure magic force at the human Vortex. Jonah Reeves raced and ducked under one blast, then another. Dammit, what was going on? He didn't have the ball. Jonah was barely participating.

He cast another shield, deflecting a particularly potent spell. Thesia screamed, denied.

"Naevys, Crete goal, maneuver three!"

Six arrows appeared in the air. Reeves stepped to the left, raised another shield above him. Naevys was across the field, to have this much range was insanity. How could she do that?

"Aaugh!"

"Oh, that's a cheap shot!" Corralee stood up in her booth, shaking a finger down at the field. Meira stood behind Reeves, looking at her two arrows lodged in his back. She nodded, and sprinted off to rejoin the battle.

"Come on, Bax! Let's get a damn call in here, the guy's bleeding."

Reeves tried to fight off the pain. He lay on his back, and just kept crawling. There wasn't a whistle, or a wind. Meira had placed the arrows well. He'd fall unconscious long before the bleeding became life-threatening. For now, he was just in agony.

Thesia straddled the human. He started to glow, wrapping as many defensive spells around himself. What was she doing? The Sun players were losing, they had to score before trying to beat him into submission.

But the elf Vortex had had enough with the score. The Bulls could take the damn Cup. She honestly had just wanted it to look good. Thanks to her idiotic team, that was impossible. The only thing left to do was show the scouts that it wasn't her fault. She was the best player, able to lead and end a game on *her* terms.

She slammed an enhanced fist down on the human's back. His shield wavered, but held. The second blow shattered it. Jonah bit his mouth shut. He'd bleed before he gave Thesia the satisfaction of his screams.

She hit him once, and again. The two teams stopped fighting, confused. There weren't the screams, the cheers from the crowd. Around the field, the fans were silent, staring towards the western goal.

A roar broke the silence. A muffled cry, and then Jonah's voice.

"Stop the match! Bax, stop the match!"

First the Bulls, then the Sun started to run towards the goal. Footsteps, hoof beats, wing beats thudded. Fewdor outpaced them all with long lumbering strides. The captains were gone, Jonah was screaming.

A whistle stopped them in their tracks.

"There, up there! Bax has called the match. The Sun has five goals, the Bulls ten, this match is over!"

The crowd erupted.

Sef and Not broke through to the goal. Airelle and Norie had already landed upon Jonah's collapsed body. Their talons were upon his back, tending to the wounds. He had lost consciousness, but seemed to be all right.

Standing by the goal was Ax. He held Thesia in his hands, engulfing the elf. He stared at her, hatred plain upon his face. His eyes burned red, hands shook. He wanted to kill her for what she had done to Jonah. No one could stop him. Maybe no one would care.

Ax set the elf down, careful to not be too rough. He turned away, and saw the rest of the Sun staring at him. Naevys and Meira's bows were out. They lowered the arrows, sheepish. The two women rushed past him to tend to their vortex.

Ruk clopped up to Ax, and stared at the tauren. Ax glared up.

"Cheap shot, what she did," Ruk murmured.

"Effective," Ax said.

"Apparently not," Ruk said. He motioned for space, and the two started to walk away. They could hear Corralee Muncie screaming the stats. Ax thought he heard his own name. Fans were probably picking their way through to rush the field.

"Wanted a second to congratulate you," Ruk said. "Before the rush of scouts."

"Scouts?" Ax tried to play it off. Ruk laughed, and nodded.

"Most likely never going to get a chance for a rematch," Ruk held up a hand before Ax could protest. "No, no. I'm losing a step, and have loved this particular league. It's smaller, but the competition has always been something to take pride in.

"Don't forget that, up there. In stadiums that will fill in the thousands for just about anything. The fans will throw themselves at your feet, kings and queens will beg your favor. The gods may call you brother, but never forget that we claimed you first. You're Ionian, and we thank you for that."

Ruk trotted away. He had said all he wanted to, and didn't hold with too much sentiment.

Ax watched the centaur leave, and didn't know how to respond. The fans were reaching the field, he could hear their roars start to reach the trees. In that mass would be one or two scouts with a missive or request for dinner later. Corralee Muncie with a great big trophy for the champions to accept.

Ionia claimed him. It didn't matter that he wasn't born there. He wasn't even a minotaur. They might kill him if they knew. A bastard of the Rus waste, a Waste Beast rather than one of the noble tauren. Lower than any of the races. Lower than humans.

Everyone wanted him. Him, Surdiax. Would they if they knew the truth?

He pushed the thought from his mind. Today, he was admired, respected. *Needed.* He was a champion, the pinnacle of achievement in all Ionia. He would rise higher, further.

He would be a god among players.

"Ax! Ax! Corralee Muncie, you just won the Ionia Cup, what do you have to say?"

"Couldn't have done it without such amazing support. Just happy to be of service."

A Girl and her Goddess

Once upon a time, a little girl found god.

Who is this girl? What caused her to start looking for gods in the first place? They were gone, centuries gone. A faint memory even before the bombs fell. When the skies burned gold and ash fell like clouds upon the world, there were no gods. Surely, as some say, there are no gods now.

Perhaps they're right. Perhaps this isn't a real tale. Perhaps gods are nothing more than a fancy, a fashion that children put on to explain the nightmares away. If they ever were real, the world is better off without such immortal titans. Simpler, more controlled. Livable.

She did find god, though. This girl found her goddess. It is a fact that will not change despite anyone's wish that it wasn't that goddess, or that girl, or that real. It just happened.

Here is how.

"Don't go out to the caves my dear,
The gods are feeling spry.
A girl in a grave is all my fear,
With gods no need to why..."

A happy poem. A children's song to help the day go by. And Bethany was a child. She had just turned seven, and was more than happy to show how many sevens she could count to.

"Jump six times,
Twirl around three,
The gods might kill you
Or invite to tea."

Bethany was never a twisted girl. This must be understood as her tale is told. She was one of the sweetest little things that anyone could ask for. From her midnight hair that curled about her face, the bright green eyes that just shone when she smiled, all the way down her favorite sundress to her toes when she ran down towards the forbidden caves.

"Don't be scared
Never flee,
The gods need us
So just let them be."

She was just always alone, that little girl. Her parents were whoever they were, and certainly never around. Bethany had friends, surely. There was no good reason for her to venture towards the caves.

There she stood before them. Far from town, far from anywhere or anyone reasonable. Bethany balanced on her toes, looking into the darkness. The single cave mouth loomed before her. It wasn't tall, but rather deep, deeper than anyone could have told dear Bethany.

"Don't go out to the caves my dear
The gods are feeling wild
They want some faith and a little blood
'specially from good young child."
"Who's out there?"

A voice. A dry voice, sardonic and coming out of the caves. The question hung liltingly in the air.

The girl peered in. "My name's Bethany."

"That's a pretty name." The voice said.

"Thank you,"

"Are you coming in?"

Bethany scuffed her feet. Was she? She wasn't entirely sure. She had come all this way, it would be a shame just to go back now.

"Ok."

She took a step forward. And then another. That wasn't so hard. Two more steps. A couple more and she was in the cave. The air grew stuffier, wet. Not cold, not hot. Just wet.

Bethany kept walking. Once she was in it was easier to just keep taking one more step. This was starting to get fun. How many steps before she reached the stairs?

She knew there would be stairs. Bethany wasn't the first to go this far. Others had, but they all turned back. And none had ever said anything about a voice.

Down the stairs, that's what everyone had said. And past the whistling hallway, that came next. And then there was a pool, Bethany knew this much at least. And there it was, black glass in the darkness. It stretched throughout a broad cavern, could have been closer to a lake than a pool.

What makes a girl go through all this to reach me? The goddess asked herself.

Jump once. Bethany landed on a rock, hidden in the still waters. She stretched as far forward as she could, trying to see the other side. It was there, there was a golden-brown light coming from the top of the cavern. She took another jump while the goddess considered.

She comes from nowhere, she is seeking nothing.

Jump again, and again. This was fun! Bethany giggled as she splashed onto the third rock. Could she do this again? She didn't even think to look down, to notice that the waters had no depths. That if she fell she would do so forever.

She brings what I desire most.

A fourth jump, then a fifth. Almost there. The last one was going to be hard, but she...made it! Bethany stood up with a smile, that did it. She wanted to catch her breath before she tried that again, but it was fun.
Faith.
"I'm ready to go again!"
"Not yet, child."
Bethany turned to look towards the light.
"What's this?"
"This was my altar."
The altar stretched almost farther than Bethany could see. Stone steps that reached up to the girl's chest, stacked towards the top of the cavern. Down one side was a long scar in the stairs, trickling down a brown sludge.
"What's that?" Bethany said, pointing.
"You don't want to know."
"Oh!" Bethany nodded. "Right, I don't like blood that much."
Strange girl.
Bethany jumped up, and scrambled on the stone steps. She slipped, fell, and landed with a dull thud. She stood up, huffed, and leaped again. The girl grabbed the stair, lost it and fell once again.
She sat against the side, and tried not to pout. It was really difficult.
"I can't get up."
The goddess' laughter trailed through the air like dust.
"Do you know what faith is, Bethany?"
The girl scrunched her face up in thought. "Is it sparkly?"
"I don't think so."
Bethany nodded. "Me neither."
She didn't know what to think. Faith was a word, or maybe even a sickness. Something the villagers got once in a while when it didn't rain, or rained too much. Or when the blacksmith's wife decided she'd rather live with the travelling merchant. They all caught faith.
This place, this is what the goddess' followers thought faith was. This edifice of granite, stretching to heavens in a cavern far beneath the earth. The immortal one could remember it all.
"They would do anything for me that they could conceive," she whispered.
Bethany cleared her throat. "I can't get up!" Bethany spoke louder this time, hoping to catch the goddess' attention.
"Oh, sweet one," The goddess said. "Think of me."
Bethany did. Hard.
"Twirl around once, and make a wish."

Bethany wished. She wished for something more than she ever had before. She never said it, or else it wouldn't come true.

"Twirl again," The goddess urged. "And consider your darkest fear."

The girl twirled, letting the sundress unfurl around her ankles. Did the air seem lighter to her? And yet less comforting? Or did she just make it so?

"One last time," The goddess whispered. "This is going to be difficult, harder than anything you've done before."

The goddess sighed. "Pray for me."

Bethany didn't speak. She just prayed once.

Her feet left the ground, and she was up! Up, up above the first steps, flying. Bethany was flying. Arms stretched out, she could twirl, and corkscrewed through the cave air.

She screamed, and giggled as the voices echoed off the walls. Her voice was a chorus, and couldn't be stopped. Bethany never wanted it to.

"This is so much fun!" Bethany screamed. She could feel the warmth from the goddess.

The goddess' attention turned to the altar. To a time when every step was filled with her followers, her faithful.

"Once I held sway over a nation that swept over these mountains. They gave me tears, torn from the sockets of virgins bent over in old age."

Bethany could spot the glow from the top of the altar. She slowed to a stop, hung above it, and sailed towards the light.

"I was serenaded in the screams of children pushed down wells. I bathed daily in the blood of thirty-seven bulls..."

Bethany lighted upon the platform – a bare surface, save for the altar. Built entirely of iron, it glowed red and golden.

"But all I wanted was faith..." The goddess' voice was wistful. In mourning.

Bethany looked around. "Where are you?

Where was the goddess? There was no one on the platform, or even atop the altar. She wasn't the glow, nothing incredible.

"Here," A voice croaked. Bethany crawled over the altar, and looked over the other side. There was nothing. No, wait! There, nestled in a crack where the iron met stone. A clay jar, a simple clay jar, the lid sealed tight.

Bethany picked up the jar, and stared at it.

"You have a big voice."

"Thank you."

This was certainly unlike anything Bethany had even dreamed about. Not even when she ran through the fields outside, thinking about the fairy kings and queens that hid on the other side of the light. None of her thoughts contained a goddess in a jar.

"Who are you?"

The clay rumbled, steam escaping from the seal.

"I am Arlyle, the Scourge of Darrenfell!" The goddess' voice shook the altar like thunder. "I laid waste to the nations of Lun'kva, and made their holy places my own! I seduced the priestesses of the Dragon Lords in a single evening. I brought the sky low and flooded the earth, to bring my people prosperity and my enemy's ruination."

The jar almost puffed up.

"I am impressive," Arlyle said.

Bethany smiled. "I'm going to call you Ari!"

"I am Arlyle, the Scourge of-"

Bethany leaned against the altar, and held the clay jar to her heart. "What can I do for you Ari?"

"Put me down!"

Bethany set the clay jar on the altar. It tottered one way, and then another. Try as it might, the jar would not topple or break apart.

"You shall refer to me as Arlyle, the Scourge of Darrenfell!" The jar shouted. "Now release me!"

Bethany plopped down next to the altar, and rested her head on the cool metal. She stared at the clay. "Why?"

The clay rumbled, threatening to burst in Bethany's face. An idle threat, to be sure.

"I am a god. I reign supreme!"

Bethany wasn't fooled. She wasn't some simple-headed child of six anymore. She was seven, and knew the ways of the world.

"You're just a jar. Or something trapped inside a jar."

Smoke flooded out of the earthenware. Arlyle flew towards the little girl, claws outstretched.

Behold, Arlyle! The demonic goddess, vengeance incarnate. Her horned crown was decorated with the skull of her most hated rival. Her face, once beauteous, was twisted into a snarl that promised everlasting agony.

"Trapped, am I?" The Scourge of Darrenfell rumbled. "Trapped in a child's dream, in her imagination?"

How dare Bethany question the Scourge's power? Did she not know how many gods Arlyle had laid low over the centuries? How her claws had tasted the flesh of countless enemies, for offenses far less grave than disobedience.

"The imagination, *your imagination*, is boundless, and the jar is only clay. Is that what you expect would hold my power? CLAY?!?"

Bethany clapped her hands, and smiled up at her goddess.

"You're weird, do you want to come out and play?"

The goddess howled in the girl's face. Wind tore at her dress, dust whirled around them in a gust. The iron altar groaned under the torrent, before splitting in the twain. The jar flew forward, straight into Bethany's waiting arms.

In an instant Arlyle was back within the jar.

"What game?"

Arlyle let out a war cry, and howled to the setting sun.

"After five centuries, I am free! You shall all once again know what it means to fear the Scourge of Darrenfell!"

She outstretched a claw forward. "The world shall bend in love!" She promised.

Bethany looked down at Arlyle. The goddess was actually smaller outside of the jar, only three feet tall. Her horned crown and skulls looked almost cute against the dusk skin of the being, her black eyes inquisitive in their fury.

The girl, however, was not amused. "This is not how you play tea party, Arlyle..."

The tiny goddess shoved her fist towards the sky. "The Scourge of Darrenfell!"

"Precisely," Bethany reached for the teapot, and poured a measure into a cracked tea cup. All the china was chipped in some form or another, but Bethany thought that just added character to the set.

"Now, enjoy your tea."

Arlyle huffed, and sat on the ground. She did sip her tea, in blessed silence.

"Much better," Bethany nodded to the doll seated on the ground next to the goddess. "Would you like to offer some tea to Miss Thraindoodle?"

"I would not," Arlyle declared. "She is a straw doll and incapable of any interaction."

The Scourge glared at the doll. "And I suspect she stuck her tongue out at me when I wasn't looking."

Bethany enjoyed her own tea with a smile. Arlyle glared at the doll, promising vengeance and fury if this slight turned out to be true. Or if Bethany wouldn't mind too much if the doll was set aflame.

But soon Arlyle looked at her own tea. Curiosity got the better of her, and she sipped again.

"I've never had a goddess before," Bethany said. "I wonder what you need to be fed."

"Blood of the…" Arlyle took another gulp, more pronounced. No… It was! "Is this tea Shaeryan Jade?"

Bethany brightened, and Arlyle cradled the cup close. "Marvelous," The goddess whispered.

The girl and her goddess both sipped their tea in silence.

"You just might be worth this, human," The goddess grudgingly let slip from her tongue.

Bethany smiled, and raised her china. "You too."

The Mad Fiddler

Listen.
Children stopped from their playing. The makeshift ball tumbled past the littlest one, hitting an oak tree. There was a sound. But it couldn't be.

No, there! There it was, lifting past the trees, from the southern mountains. It was louder now, higher than the winds. A farmer looked up. His wheat hung from the stalks. If it didn't get cut soon, it might be lost in a rain. But if the sound was real, then maybe, just maybe, it was too much to consider.

A long trill sailed through the trees. That was it! That was his mark! He was coming, the Fiddler was coming. The children screamed, and ran past the farmer to the trees. The sturdy workman leaned on his scythe and looked on.

Before the kids had reached the tree line, there he was. Bursting through the foliage in a flash of crimson, there he was. Tapping a rhythm on one buckled dance shoe, he struts towards the children. His cloak hung in tatters on his shoulders. His doublet was embossed, with silver pins down the side of every seam, matching the curled hair that hung about a beaming face.

And the fiddle, oh, the fiddle! The Blackwood sparkled in the fading light. And when that golden bow did its own dance upon the strings, that sound travelled throughout the village. More and more heads, far beyond the children and the farmer, knew what was coming next.

The mad Fiddler was in town!

He spun again, letting the cloak tease the children. They squealed, and fell in line behind him. The Fiddler struck another note, and hummed a counterpoint. Then came the second, and third. He tapped against the dirt path twice, and off he went, little ones in tow.

The farmer watched the spectacle, the cloak flapping in the wind. He looked at his scythe, and up at the cloudless sky. The farm tool spun to the ground as he raced to keep up.

The farmer wasn't alone. The blacksmith barely had enough time to blow out the furnace before he lost his place to the baker and her assistant. There was little Mrs. Tafitha

coming down from her bowery. No one wanted to be left behind, the Fiddler was here. His song meant dance, and song, and food.

He spun his way through town. For those who didn't join fast enough, he slowed the pace. Anyone who looked too glum or angered, he would circle once, and with one verse of nonsense the offending grimace was gone, and off the mass of dancers would go again.

The Fiddler reached the edge of town. Any who had not followed him were either out of reach, or were at the manse ahead. He stopped, tapped twice, and the crowd fell silent.

His eyes scanned the townsfolk. Old, young, elf, fae and human all stared back. The mad Fiddler was known for outbursts, but never on the poor. And the Baron had always been kind enough to ensure the town's destitute nature remained in place.

The corner of the musician's mouth twitched. He let it grow into a smile.

"Let's find the Baron," He murmured.

Find the Baron! They'd follow this man right out of town. He pirouetted and leaped up on the steps, his fiddle already hard at work defining the tune. Keeping time with the clack of his shoes on the stones, a sprint could not keep up with him.

The line burst apart, too full of dance and vigor to be contained. Children were swept up by mothers and fathers, most oft not their own, and there they would go. Up the steps, past the run-down cobble to the more refined granite as they neared the manse. The young danced on the balconies, adults swooping next to them. Yippees, cries and yelps could burst forth at any moment, the Fiddler was here!

The Fiddler was here. At the top of the steps the guards tightened their grips on the golden gate. Swords were tucked behind their velvet cloaks, rattling in their scabbards. At the sound the Fiddler quickened his pace, matching the beat as he scuttled towards them. He dipped low, and bowed in one long note on the fattest string. Then silence.

The guards could not see the end of the crowd. The townsfolk leaned one way or another, jumping on offered shoulders to catch a glimpse of the hold-up up front. There was to be a party, who was trying to stop this? Not these two, certainly.

The Fiddler spun his bow, and tucked it away up his sleeve. He leaned up against the bars, and smiled.

"Dear gentlemen," His voice was a whisper, yet it carried to every soul on the steps. "I have crossed mountain and dale and quickening river to reach your fine abode. In celebration, these fine folks desire, nay, require merriment. They have all worked so hard, and are all assembled for your convenience."

He flashed his most dazzling smile towards the guardsmen. "May we demand entrance?"

They thought about denial. Truly, the words were on the tips of their tongues. Perhaps the words were even spoken as the gates were opened. They perhaps even spoke the words as the crowd filed past. But not before the Mad Fiddler had left earshot.

"No?" Apparently he had indeed heard the words, whispered amidst the heavy footsteps and happy twittering of the celebrants. There he was, slid in between the two swordsmen with a whisper.

"Which one spoke no?" The myth leaned on their shoulders. The fiddle hung on his back, silently accusing.

The fiddler grabbed the ear to his left. "Lend me that for a moment," He muttered into the appendage. "You have been very kind in listening to a humble performance by this insane one and his fine bow. But the mouth attached to you needs to be shut before it is corrected.

"And you," He twisted the ear of the second guard. The man cried out, a burst before the fiddler clamped a hand over his mouth. "That mouth sounds closer, but I'm not sure if it was offensive. Just smells as such."

The Mad Fiddler let go of ear and mouth, before holding both guards' hands in his own. "Now you, fair ladies," He crooned. "Your work in this finery is without compare. I would not deprive the world of you, even to remove those most odious mouths and the rancid teeth within."

He bowed low. "Your hands have pled your case masterfully, gentlemen. I will not take your mouths this day. Now, smart up!"

The guards fell into line. The fiddler pat the hands again, treasuring the moment. Then he was off again. Perhaps the Baron would be a finer gentleman than his guards' mouths.

The Baron at the moment was wondering if he could escape. An obese man for his small stature, his clothes almost bled purple onto the marble floors as he quivered in the main hall. He scratched a mass of tangled wisps upon his scalp, and eyes darted this way or that. There were dignitaries and minor members of the nobility surrounding him, not that he cared. The Mad Fiddler was here.

What were the options before the ruler? He could try and burst through the front doors, trample those too slow or too stupid to allow him egress. Or perhaps shield his girth behind his loyal, heftier subjects, that could work. Or even, yes, maybe have the guards stop the Fiddler before he got close! Let them risk their lives. That could work.

That couldn't work. Many had tried to deny the Fiddler his festivities. Their fates ran fast before the musician's footsteps. The very thought of his exploits had sent many of the dignitaries with weak stomachs to the lavatories. And he had breached the walls.

The rich could hear his mob now. The rabble milled about the hallways, and they just remained there. Tracking dirt into the carpets, wiping their filthy hands on the artwork. There might even be some sneezing that could contaminate the very air. And anyone with the power to stop them was trapped in the chamber.

The poor dared not venture into the main hall. The Fiddler would make his own entrance, in his own time. He needed to hurry up and get it over with.

Once he moved, he moved! The Fiddler swept through the doors, shook the oak frames as the gold-inlay scraped across the marble floors. He stood proudly, one foot cocked just so to allow his full frame maximum view to his audience. He trilled his instrument, and danced for all to see.

"Dance, my fair-haired pack of vermin!" He cried out. "Dance for the song in your hearts, and the fear in your bones, for the Fiddler has come with festive in his soul!"

Did they dance? There was nothing that could have stopped them! Once-proud gentlemen swept their ladies off their feet, intent on proving themselves the most able on the floor. Never mind that particular dancing was last year's fashion. The Fiddler was here!

He looked towards the Baron. The noble had stood rooted to the spot, knees quivering in anticipation as his dignitaries waltzed around him. Was he supposed to dance? Was he to be singled out for an example? What was to happen to him?

The Fiddler slowed down the pace, letting the waltz become more natural. The dancing court soon found its tempo and followed along. They tried to regain some of their stately composure. The musician for his part lounged in the Baron's chair, letting his music sail from high notes to low.

He had taken his eyes off the Baron, pensively staring at his own buckled shoes. He kicked once, and then again. Then the music stopped.

Everyone stood still, and looked at the Fiddler. He stretched, languid on the chair. He overbalanced, and tumbled headfirst off the arm. The musician somersaulted, and was back on his feet in an instant, all smiles and laughter. The fiddle and bow were none the worse for wear.

"That's better," He said. "Now…shall we gather the rest of the guests?"

Time flew by without thought or reason. The Fiddler picked up his bow once again, and the partygoers all left the banquet hall. It never would have fit the entire town. Besides, a party like this deserved the open air.

Out there, out on the great lawn. Behind the manse, surrounded by gardens and a wondrous hedge maze. Many of the townsfolk had never seen such a place. They could be seen standing on the back steps, just for a moment, taking in the sights, the smells. The sounds were all provided by him.

First would be the food. It was a curious thing, the food. The servants were not expected to provide, they were standing next to their fellow man, or dancing as the case may be. The nobles certainly did not cook and serve, it was much too succulent. None took too long thinking of how such confections appeared. When they appeared on long tables arranged on the lawn, the people ate. When they finished, it was assumed they would be gone.

Dinner was uneventful. At least, it was supposed to be. The Fiddler was serenading a group of ladies and their spouses, when a particularly exuberant gentlemen stood up, anxious to show off. He held his glass high, red-faced and triumphant.

"A toast!" He shouted, interrupting the Fiddler's piece. "To the Mad Fiddler. The greatest bastards these poor schmucks could ever hope for!"

A silence fell over the crowd. Silverware was dropped on plates, glasses carefully set down. The ladies the gentlemen hoped to win over wanted very much to run away.

The Fiddler, for his part, stopped playing. He stared ahead, curious. He nodded once, and set down his instrument on the table. He poured himself a glass of wine from the gentlemen's bottle.

"Very well, a toast." He held his glass high. "What shall it be? To madness, or perhaps music? A madness this be, vibrated air that kills sorrow as oft as it births pain. May I, a humble fool, be its embodiment."

"Hear, hear!" The drunkard said.

The Fiddler sipped once while his companion downed the drink.

"This is a Malbec," The bard commented.

"The fine-" The last of the words were lost in strangled gasps of air. The Fiddler stabbed forward, shattering the glass in the man's throat. He stabbed once, and again, his face a mask of fury.

"You do not serve a Malbec before dancing!" He punctuated each word with another blow. "It makes the guests lethargic!"

The now-dead man was in no position to respond or defend his selection. The Fiddler stared down at the shattered glass, dripping dregs of wine and blood.

He took a curious taste, and nodded. "There, a harsher bite, not heavy. Keeps the mind awake, if not too sharp. Perfect for dancing."

The Fiddler, instrument in hand once more, bowed low to the ladies. "May I interest these fine guests in perhaps a twostep?"

Yes, he was mad. But then, he was also right about the wine choice.

The Fiddler was hard to understand. As the night progressed, and the body rolled away, the Fiddler watched it all with mirth, accompanying even the procession with a dirge. The patrons soon forgot the tragedy as the dancing progressed without further incident. There was too much joy to be found to dwell on one sorrow.

He was in the thick of it all. There was not a lass whose hand was not graced with his lips, nor a man's for that matter. He played games with the children, told the best lewd stories with the elders, and at the end of the night painted the great sculptures crimson in stale wine.

The dancing was many and varied. Could one really describe the steps made, the gestures, and the movement? None of these townsfolk were what could be even generously described as fine dancers. Yet they, in that motion, were perfect. Every single one of them. It had to be the Fiddler, though how he would never say.

The festivities lasted for days, or hours, eternally or possibly it didn't last at all. Once it was done, there it was gone. The platters once piled high with bones and refuse had been cleared away, the tables returned to their halls. There was just an entire town, ready to retire.

They all filed out in their own separate way together. The butcher and baker helped their husbands into bed. The Baron himself was seen helping many a child find their way home to parents who had lost them in the shuffle. No one was lost, and there was a pillow ready and waiting for each restive head.

The Fiddler sat on the steps leading down from the manse, playing a lullaby for all. The guards were in bed, given a respite. There would be no trouble, not tonight, that was for tomorrow. Tonight there was a soothing song, sailing on the night breeze.

The Fiddler did not stop until all were abed. Not until every light winked out, a final salute to his work. Then he lifted the bow from the fiddle, tucked them both behind his back, and started off towards the next village. In the morning the Baron would find

his coffers drained, but not egregiously. He might even wonder if he were truly angry at such blatant thievery.

What to make of the Fiddler? It is not as if he cared one way or another. This was as he always comported himself. He neither asked permission or advice, nor did he seem to give any. He was more a force than a man. Perhaps that is what he hopes we all think.

He's still out there, somewhere. Stirring up a song and dance, ready to beat rhythm into an unsuspecting noble. Wonder when he'll come here.

A Prayer for the Thirteen

To all the gods and none. To all those who may give solace to those who died, we pray now. May any who may be listening, hear these prayers.

The Elements
We give thanks to those who gave us the elements. Those who fell in the Sphere of Five were held fast, to the ever turbulent call of nature.

A Prayer to Mumbai
To the city of earth, the churning ground,
Ageless, unchanging, yet new
The folly that this land found
Showed strength, and virtue was their due

A Prayer to Rome
To the city of fire, city of red
Twice blessed to rule the earth
In fire it was born, in fire it bled
In fire it found its worth

A Prayer to Tokyo
To the city of air, not of flight
Honor was the land's core
The Folly came, and in its light
They died, but still they soar.

A Prayer to Sydney
To the city of water, return
A city that could forgive
Past sins were gone, would not burn
Be an example again, relive.

A Prayer to New York
To the city of iron, structures tall
The first of the new land
Forged in war, when fires fall
They made the final stand.

The Directions

We pray today in all directions, so that all who have fallen can be seen, felt, and answered.

A Prayer to Beijiing
Look to the East, the Risen Sun
To those who once held sway
We give thanks those who had begun
The journey, and gave light to day.

A Prayer to Johannesberg
Look to the South, in blackened ash
The flames that beat the earth
To those who had no hand in this clash
May you find a resting hearth

A Prayer to Los Angeles
Look to the west, onset of Night
Second city to the second land
For those who once made future bright
And died with promises in hand

A Prayer to Moscow
Look to the North, the Frozen time
Unbent, defiant to the last
To those whose heart heard not the chime
As they faded towards the past

The Body of the World

A prayer to the measures of each man, woman and child who fell. Let the merits of these bodies be examples to us now.

A Prayer to London
To those who led with reasoned mind
Calloused from the whims of heart
Towards magic, they may be blind
But their feats shall not depart

A Prayer to Rio de Janeiro
To those who moved with passion
With open hearts and love
We show our thanks for their compassion
To all who felt wrath from above.

A Prayer to Jerusalem
This, above all, held the sway
Beyond reason, rhyme and song
The gods have returned, here to stay

We confirm, you were never wrong

And always the unknown. Though Never there.

A last repose, a final care.

Gods, Goddesses, those who give aid.
Grant us this mercy, this we pray.

Jack Holder

The Writer

A Master's Student at Boston University, Jack spends his days wandering between one fantasy world and another that is just a bit closer to reality. He has never been abducted by aliens, does not have an evil twin, and contrary to popular belief was not the culprit of the Great Pudding Wars of 1935.

He also says thank you, a lot.

About the Artists

James Bardes
Post-Apocalyptic Flooding, The Last Bullet, The Ax Rises
James is a self-taught artist and Star Wars fanatic. His early influences were from fantasy illustrators: Larry Elmore, Clyde Caldwell, Keith Parkinson, Jeff Miracola, Janet Aulisio, Tony DiTerlizzi. He uses a blend of traditional and digital mediums, specializing in pencil and ink. His art has been featured in the Eldritch fantasy roleplaying game system by Dan Cross from Crossroad Games. He resides in New York City with his wife and son, the primary sources of his inspiration. James can always be reached at bardicdesignstudios@gmail.com

Ed Bickford
Promethean Sparks, A Girl and her Goddess, A Family Far Beneath the Stars
Ed Bickford has been drawing since he can remember. He served his country in the United States Air Force for 10 years. He had always wanted to go to college for art and one day he was able to use his G.I. Bill to attend college for Illustration. Ed has self published books and has been published by a few indie publishers.

He lives in Kansas city with his 3 kids and his wife and 2 dogs. If you're reading this, he is probably drawing at this moment.
http://www.edbickford.com/

Carlos Bonardi
Lost Heroines
An illustrator, graphic/web and interactive infographics designer, Carlos Bonardi lives in Buenos Aires, Argentina. Carlos loves everything that has to do with the world of creativity, illustration, design, comics, computer graphics, animation, interactivity, video games, toys, art, books, and magazines.
Since his childhood he liked to make up stories, fantastic storytelling where art poured forth. Cartoons from the 80's, He-Man toys, comic books and video games no doubt influenced his future career choice. With all that influence he studied graphic and graduated from the American University. In parallel he took workshops in illustration and cartoons.
Carlos has worked for over 4 years at lanacion.com generating content for newspaper articles with illustrations, infographics, interactive multimedia specials, entertainment and anything that has to do with web design and programming.
Carlos' web page is www.carlosbonardi.com.ar and can be reached at the Twitter handle @carlosbonardi

Phoebe Herring
Cover Artist
Phoebe is a concept artist and illustrator with a love of Fantasy art. She takes her inspiration from Cornwall's elemental landscape. She has worked on a variety of creative projects across publishing, games and animation. She lectures on concept art at Falmouth University.

wild

Her work can be viewed at www.phoebeherring.com

Cari Dee

Mars: Year 1

"The INDIE Comics are less mainstream and raw, I want to be a part of it, I want to make one...and finally make MORE."

Cari Dee is a graduate of Fine Arts Major in Advertising in the Philippines. She is currently a freelance artist/illustrator who played a big role in the creative design of Mongrel City, her first Comic stint which was released last July of this year. She is a graphics artist who specializes in Traditional pencil drawing, Logo design and Character concepts. Her vibe and style in her creative designs has been well received and was able to jumpstart her career in the world of Comics Design.

This is not giving you enough details, let her art show you more, follow her at: https://www.facebook.com/DeeviousArt/

Saint Yak

Proper War, Mad Fiddler

The 35 year old artist lives in Moscow with wife, son and cat. A staple in the indie comics industry, he is part of the new graphic novel "Go West," "1% Life – Die to Ride," and others. His favorite artists and influences include Sean Gordon Murphy, Tony Moore, Dustin Nguyen, Bill Sienkiewicz and our Lord and savior Jim Lee.

His work can be found on www.saintyak.deviantart.com and on Facebook at Saint Yak.

Made in the
USA
Middletown, DE